THE OTHER SIDE OF THE HUDSON

The Do-It-Yourself
Jewish Adventure Series
by Kenneth Roseman

THE CARDINAL'S SNUFFBOX

THE MELTING POT: *An Adventure in New York*

ESCAPE FROM THE HOLOCAUST

THE TENTH OF AV

THE OTHER SIDE OF THE HUDSON: *A Jewish Immigrant Adventure*

THE OTHER SIDE OF THE HUDSON

A Jewish Immigrant Adventure

KENNETH ROSEMAN

◆ ◆ ◆

UAHC Press
New York

To Dr. Nelson Glueck

This is the Torah that Moses placed before the Israelites . . . on the other side of the Jordan. . . .

(Deuteronomy 4: 44, 46)

Maps by Bill Cwiekalo.

Photographs, courtesy of the American Jewish Archives, Hebrew Union College-Jewish Institute of Religion, Cincinnati, Ohio (cover, pp. 28, 36, 42, 52, 58, 66, and 108).

Library of Congress Cataloging-in-Publication Data
Roseman, Kenneth.
    The other side of the Hudson / Kenneth Roseman.
      p. cm. — (Do-it-yourself Jewish adventure series)
    Includes bibliographical references.
    Summary: As a young Jewish immigrant from Bavaria in the mid-nineteenth century, the reader makes decisions that mirror the choices made by new Jewish Americans as they settled in the United States.
    ISBN 0-8074-0506-X (acid-free paper)
    1. Jews—United States—History—19th century—Juvenile fiction.
2. Plot-your-own stories. [1. Jews—United States—Fiction.
2. Emigration and immigration—Fiction. 3. Plot-your-own stories.]
I. Title. II. Series.
PZ7.R718630t   1993
[Fic]—dc20
                                            93-33138
                                             CIP
                                           AC

1

Strap on your spurs and six-shooters. Get ready to ride steam-puffing trains and sailing ships. Prepare to fight off yellow fever epidemics, to wrestle with questions about slavery, to start your own business, and to succeed or fail as you make your way in America. Gather up your courage for some great adventures!

Between 1850 and 1880, the Jewish population of America grew from approximately 50,000 to 250,000. Much of this increase came from immigration, and most of these new immigrants came from Germany and other parts of central Europe. The arrivals were often young—frequently teenagers—and they were determined to make a new life for themselves in this new world of North America. Most of them succeeded remarkably well.

When they arrived in this country, they had two tasks: to find out what American life was all about and to become part of it and still remain Jewish. As you read this book, you, too, will experience America west of the Hudson River during this exciting period. The events in this book are based on the true-life adventures of Jewish immigrants in an expanding America.

2

One of the greatest challenges facing you is the creation of an American-Jewish community and style of life. Jews settled all over the country. During these years many of the great Jewish institutions in America were established. In fact, very few major Jewish communities were founded after this period. Jews developed specifically American forms of Judaism and Jewish charities, hospitals, clubs, and other organizations. It is this creative and exciting time you are about to enter.

This book is about history and choices people made as they faced real problems and challenges. They had to make decisions—the same decisions you will make as you read this book. The choices they made shaped American-Jewish history and the lives of Jews in this country.

In making your decisions, you will select one option over another. What will determine your choice? Most of the time, one option will appear better than the other. Usually decisions are based on what we call "values." As you read the book, think about the "whys" or "values" that will guide you in making your choices.

3

Y ou may have already learned in your own life that what seems a very good choice may not turn out well. And, sometimes, if you get lucky, a bad choice can come out fine. At other times, one option seems no better than another. Just flip a coin and take whatever comes up. These possibilities also occurred in history, and you should think about them as you create your own historical adventures.

As you find words in *italics,* look them up in the glossary at the back of the book.

When you find the names of places in the United States and Canada, look them up on the map and Map Key on pages 138 and 139. Places outside North America will appear on the maps on page 140.

Get ready to move back through time. You are about to become a Jewish immigrant, arriving from Bavaria in 1851, anxious to make a new life on the American frontier. You're going to have some fabulous adventures and some unpredictable experiences—it's never going to be dull. Now turn to page 4 to begin the story.

4

As soon as Papa opened the front door that evening, you knew that something was wrong. A deep frown covered his face, and his back was bent over as though he were carrying a heavy weight on his shoulders. You, your two younger sisters, and your mother ran to the door. "What's wrong? What has happened?" Papa hung his heavy woolen coat on the hook and pulled off his boots. Each boot fell to the ground with a thud, and you felt that this muffled sound echoed the sadness deep inside Papa. It took quite a while before he was able to speak.

Finally, he said, "A terrible thing happened today. You know that every week I go to the city, buy cloth, and bring it home. For nearly twelve hours each day, I sit in this room and make shirts, one at a time. I cut the pieces out of the cloth and carefully sew them together. If I sew quickly, I can make three or four shirts in a day. Then, when all the cloth is used up, I take the finished shirts back to the city, sell them in the marketplace, and buy more cloth. Usually, I have enough money left over to pay for our food and the other things we need.

"Today, a rich man from Berlin came to our city and opened a shirt factory. Tailors like me no longer will be able to make shirts at home. We shall have to go to the factory in the morning and work there all day. Each worker will make only a little piece of each shirt so the work will go faster. The factory will be able to finish hundreds of shirts each day ... faster ... cheaper ... with fewer workers. I tried to get a job in the factory, but I was told that they had already hired all the workers they need. I cannot earn money. I do not know how we shall manage."

5

After dinner, Papa and Mama talked for a long time. You could hear their voices but couldn't understand what they were saying because they were crying. Finally, they called for you.

"Our dearest, oldest child," they said. "We have had to make a very difficult decision. There is no future for you in Germany. Even if Papa gets a job, there will not be enough money to support our family. Do you remember the Felfass family from Floss? Do you remember that they sent their children, one by one, to America and how each child found a job there, saved money, and sent it back so that the next member of the family could also go to America? You have grown up here in Neustadt, but now you must begin a long journey, the longest trip of your life, a trip to the new world of America. We shall buy your ticket tomorrow and help you all we can. You are really not old enough to leave us, but we have no choice; you must go."

And so, one winter morning, you left Neustadt, journeying by train to Hamburg and then on a sailing ship to New York City. On your trip across the Atlantic Ocean in the middle of winter, it was freezing cold, and the ocean waves were rough. You were sick most of the way across, as were many of the other passengers, Jews like yourself who could no longer find a way to live in German lands.

6

On the second night of *Chanukah* in the year 1851 (5612 on the Hebrew calendar), you arrive in the port of New York. This is the largest city you have ever seen. When you get off the ship, you walk and walk, up and down the wide, long streets, looking into every shop window, watching all the different people.

But something bothers you. The city is too big, too noisy, too crowded. You have grown up outside the small city of Neustadt, and you feel more at home in a small place. You talk with some other Jewish people who have lived in New York for some time, and they suggest you might be happier living somewhere else, perhaps on the other side of the Hudson. Two options present themselves. You weigh them seriously and finally make a choice about the direction in which you will travel.

If you elect to go north, up the Hudson River toward Albany,
turn to page 8.

If you prefer to go south, traveling by ship along the coast toward Savannah, Georgia,
turn to page 9.

7

There certainly is more to life than entering numbers in a ledger. After work, you go back to the boarding house where you live with about ten other young German-Jewish men. Dinner is almost always a large pot of stew and biscuits, accompanied by pitchers of beer. After dinner, you go out to the pump in the garden to draw some fresh, cold water. You wash up and then head for the Young Men's Literary Society. It sounds dull, but the discussions are exciting to you. Tonight, one of the members plans to attack the very factory system in which you work. You imagine he will say it deprives hardworking men and women of the satisfaction of finishing one shirt at a time. True, you think to yourself, but Fechheimer has been very good to me. I wonder how I will respond.

After several years at Fechheimer's, you talk to Mr. Fechheimer about finding a more responsible job. He suggests you become a peddler, carrying his shirts from farmhouse to farmhouse, selling them to people who live away from Cincinnati.

On the other hand, *Rabbi Isaac Mayer Wise* still holds an attraction for you, as he does for many others in the city. You often think about him and about what he is trying to accomplish.

If you decide to become a door-to-door shirt peddler for Fechheimer's, turn to page 57.

If you choose to follow the lead of Rabbi Wise and study to become a rabbi in Cincinnati, turn to page 64.

8

Yelling back and forth, deckhands cast off the lines that hold your ship to the dock. Huge paddle wheels on each side of the ship begin to turn. You're on your way north, up the Hudson River toward Albany.

A thick black cloud gushes up from the two tall smokestacks. Deep within the ship, men throw wood on the fire that heats the water that makes the steam that turns the wheels that push your ship upriver against the current. Soot and smoke cover you and everyone standing near you. Some passengers joke that you look like *Negroes.* Their comments are ugly, and you think to yourself: What a strange country! The Declaration of Independence says that "all men are created equal," but, obviously, some people must be more equal than others. You move away from these people.

Later that afternoon, you notice a man standing at the ship's rail. He is crying. Hearing him moan some words in *Yiddish,* you approach him, asking, "Is there something wrong?" "Oy," he replies, "I have just lost my life." "How can that be?" you ask. "Before I left New York, a friend wrote out for me all the English words I would need in America. While I was trying to learn them, the piece of paper blew out of my hands and fell into the river. I have just lost my life." You tell him his life is not lost. You assure him that he will find Jews in Albany who will help him learn English. He dries his tears and smiles a bit. You have done a small *mitzvah*—but a *mitzvah* nonetheless.

If, after arriving in Albany, you decide to remain there,
turn to page 10.

If you prefer to continue westward,
turn to page 11.

9

Sails flutter down from the tall masts as your ship turns south on the Hudson River and down the Atlantic coast. After ten days, your ship enters the Savannah River and slowly glides up to the dock at Factor's Walk. You go ashore and walk up the tree-lined streets. The great oaks are covered with gray-green Spanish moss; it gives the city something of an eerie look. Every few blocks, there is a lovely, little open square, a park, surrounded by stately, pillared homes. You walk from one square to another until you see Congregation Mickve Israel.

You enter this very old synagogue, one of the five original congregations that existed in this country at the time of the Revolutionary War. It is Saturday. The worshipers are just finishing their morning service, and you join in the parts you know. Afterwards, several men introduce themselves and their families to you. "You're welcome here, but what are your plans for the future?" Good question. Three of the men make suggestions that you think you should take seriously. One tells of good jobs in Georgia, in small towns away from the seacoast. Another suggests going on to New Orleans, referring to that city as the capital of the new South. A third shouts, "California has lots of gold. Why waste time here. Go there at once."

If you decide to stay in Georgia, inland away from the coast,
turn to page 12.

If you decide to continue on to New Orleans,
turn to page 13.

If you decide to go to California,
turn to page 14.

10

At services on *Shabbat* morning, the slender, young, balding rabbi comes to the *bimah.* He turns to the congregation and announces: "Today, we are trying something new. Today, we have an organ to play our music."

A heavyset, older man rises from his seat. He marches deliberately, angrily toward the rabbi. "Rabbi Wise, no one gave you the right to change the *minhag* of our congregation. We have never had a musical instrument on *Shabbos,* and as long as I am president we won't." Isaac Mayer Wise is not a rabbi to back away from an argument, but what happens next is more than anyone expected. The two men begin to hit each other, fighting over the right to change the music of the services. Wise, however, is no match for his opponent. With blood running down from his nose, he leaves the temple.

After services, you leave, too. It is clear you cannot stay in a town where change is resisted so strongly. You came to America to make a change in your life. If these people protest such a minor change as in the music of the service, you know they will oppose other changes you would like to see. Where will you go?

*If you decide to go to Cleveland, Ohio,
where, you have heard, there is a growing
Jewish community,
turn to page 40.*

*If you decide to follow Rabbi Isaac Mayer
Wise to his new post in Cincinnati, Ohio, at
the other end of the state,
turn to page 41.*

11

Up the valley of the Mohawk River, along the Erie Canal, you make your way westward. At Buffalo, some of the Jews who live there take you on an outing to the St. Lawrence River. At Grand Island, they explain that it was here that *Mordecai Manuel Noah* once tried to set up a Jewish settlement called Ararat. "He wanted to create an ideal community, a place where Jews could come to live in peace and harmony," they tell you. "Of course, it didn't work. Hardly anybody moved out here. That was over twenty-five years ago, and this was really wilderness then. Indians were about the only people who would live on Grand Island at that time."

The idea of a Jew who followed his dreams intrigues you. You are young. If you're going to reach for adventure, this is certainly the time in your life to do it.

Some books you have read tell stories about fur traders who live and travel during the summer among the Indians of Canada. What an exciting life they must live, you think to yourself. I'd really like to try something like that.

On the other hand, you've never lived out in the wilderness. Perhaps you ought to be a little more cautious and head for Chicago, a city ripe for adventure, but still a city.

If you choose to live and travel among the Indians of Canada, turn to page 36.

If you decide to continue toward the West and Chicago, turn to page 37.

12

The man who tells you about the jobs available inland in Georgia introduces you to another man. He is in Savannah to pick up goods that came on your ship and take them back to his store in Talbottom. The trip covers several hundred miles, and he indicates that he could use your help, not only in transporting his merchandise, but also in selling it when it arrives at its destination.

Since there aren't a lot of other jobs available, you agree to accompany *Lazarus Straus* back to this small Georgia town and to work for him there. It's about as far from Neustadt as you can possibly imagine, but, since the Strauses are also German-Jewish immigrants, you have something in common. If they made it, so can you!

Straus helps you learn about his business and how to speak a little English. Then he gives you a horse and a wagon loaded with various kinds of merchandise. "Go from house to house. Tell them what you have to sell. Most of them will be glad to buy whatever you have." And that's what you do.

As you peddle through southwest Georgia, you realize that your customers rely on you also for news.
If this gives you an idea for another career,
turn to page 45.

If, after several years, feeling very much a southerner, you come to like this way of life,
turn to page 46.

13

Later, the man who suggested you go to New Orleans tells you that trouble is coming to the Old South. There may even be war. It would be safer and smarter to get out, to go west, and to make a new life for yourself.

That's good advice, and you quickly reboard the ship. It sails southward around the tip of Florida and through the Caribbean. After about ten days, it docks on the levees that keep the Mississippi River floods from drowning the city of New Orleans.

What a different place this is! Savannah was English; New Orleans is French. It was only a few years ago that the pirate Jean Lafitte prowled the bayous in his fast boats, darting out to capture prizes and terrorize ships' crews. Lafitte is gone now, but the French influence is still here. Even the way they speak English is different; you can hardly understand what they are saying.

As in Savannah, you go first to the synagogue. What better place to meet Jewish people and to find out what you can do in New Orleans! As in Savannah, you find no lack of advice. Some people urge you to stay in New Orleans to help establish a home for Jewish orphans. Others tell you about some arguments in the community that are truly frightening.

If you decide to stay in New Orleans to perform the mitzvah of helping establish the orphan home,
turn to page 43.

If you choose to hear more about the frightening community arguments,
turn to page 44.

14

The oldest of the three men with whom you speak takes you aside. "You are young, my friend. I myself was young once. But I was stupid. I could have gone to new places, done exciting things, had great adventures. But I listened to cautious people. I stayed here, went into the same business as my father, married the woman they picked out for me, did as I was told. Now that I am old, I look back. It has been a good life but a boring life. If I were you, I would not hesitate for a second. Go to California! Take a chance or two! What have you to lose? When you're older, you can settle down."

As you think about the alternatives—working as a store clerk in central Georgia or going to Mobile or New Orleans—you realize that the man's ideas make more and more sense. If you're ever going to take a risk, now is the time.

You go back to Factor's Walk and talk to some of the sailors. One boat is leaving directly for California. It will sail around Cape Horn, a very long voyage, but directly to San Francisco. Other sailors urge you to take a ship to Panama, walk across the Isthmus, and then take another ship up the west coast.

If you decide to take the ship that will sail around Cape Horn directly to San Francisco, turn to page 38.

If you choose to take the ship to Panama, walk across the Isthmus, and then take another ship up the west coast, turn to page 39.

15

Many of Cleveland's Jews come from the Hungarian city of Budapest. In 1848, many Hungarians had hoped that the government would allow them to vote, to have a parliament, to be able to help decide how their lives would go. But the rulers of Hungary opposed these changes; they were unwilling to share their power with those who wanted democracy. Those who protested were ruthlessly crushed by the army. Many hid, but most were caught and imprisoned. Many people left the country, including Jews who later settled in Cleveland.

Still, they are very much like the German Jews of the city. They speak German, enjoy the same music, poetry, and dances as the Germans, even pray from the same prayer book. There are differences. Their food is spicier; they love paprika and a delicious fruit-filled dessert called strudel. But, overall, they and the German Jews of Cleveland get along well. On *Shabbat* morning, they all gather at a small building they have rented for their synagogue. The sign outside says *Anshe Chesed Congregation*. From the size of the crowd, soon they will have to find a bigger place. Cleveland, you are certain, will be a major Jewish community, and you are glad you decided to remain here.

The only question is: What will you do? How will you support yourself? One Saturday evening after *Havdalah,* your friends yell, argue, laugh, debate; everyone knows what would be best for you to do. Finally, you stop the discussion. "It seems," you conclude, "that there are really only two good ideas: Either I can find a job in a factory, or I can move out to 'The Heights' and try my luck on a farm."

*If you decide to look for a factory job,
turn to page 47.*

16

If you choose to become a farmer, remembering the clean air of Neustadt, turn to page 48.

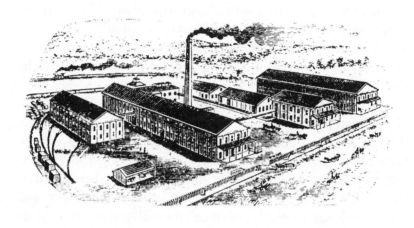

17

Circleville is a lovely farm town in the middle of Ohio's rolling hills. The people who live there are friendly and honest. You could live here comfortably. You find a job keeping the ledgers and other records at the small bank in town and settle down. Everything seems to be going well.

There is only one problem. As far as you know, you are the only Jew in Circleville. There certainly is no synagogue; the closest one is in Columbus. You go there for the *High Holy Days* and *Pesach,* but it's not the same as being able to spend every Sabbath with a congregation of your own people.

The man you work for at the bank is an elder in the Methodist church. He understands how lonely you feel and invites you to come to church with him. He tells you that no one will try to convert you, but you are suspicious. Still, you feel a deep need to pray to God, and the Methodists you know are fine and decent people. True to the banker's word, no one pressures you. It's better than not going anywhere at all.

Still, in the quiet of your room, you recognize that there must be more to life than keeping the books of a small bank in a small town. You want more out of life. Perhaps you ought to enroll at one of the nearby colleges. On the other hand, maybe you should open a store.

If you decide to enroll in a nearby college,
turn to page 51.

If you choose to open a store,
turn to page 52.

18

Great deposits of iron ore have been discovered in the Mesabi Range of Minnesota. A town, Virginia, has sprung up. All around it, mining has begun, stripping the soil away and then hauling the iron ore out in mule-driven wagons. The wagons move day and night, a steady stream winding out of the region and down to Duluth. There the ore is placed in ships bound for mills that are being built near Chicago.

You have no interest in mining. It is very difficult and awfully dangerous work. But, you notice that the miners have lots of money to spend every weekend, and it is that which attracts you to the area.

You use the money that you saved from the fur trade to establish a general store and trading post. Men come in from the mines. They need all sorts of basic things: clothing, razors, pots and pans, presents for their lady friends—almost anything. And they need a place to stay and eat. Soon, the upstairs of your store becomes a boarding house, and a new annex behind the store rises to become a saloon and restaurant.

However, you cannot handle this increased business alone. As you see it, you have two options.

If you decide to stay, finding people to help you,
turn to page 55.

If you choose to sell the business, make a profit, and move,
turn to page 61.

19

Milwaukee is a German city. Although it's located on Lake Michigan in the middle of America, it is really German. As you walk along the Milwaukee River in the evening, you can hear German singing from the beer gardens that line the streets. In Catholic and Protestant churches and in the synagogue, during the services, German is more likely to be used than English. Almost all the thousand or so Jews who live in the city come from Germany, and a steady stream of new immigrants, often family members, joins them. Milwaukee is a thriving, growing community, and you know that there must be many opportunities for an energetic, strong, young person like you.

One day, as you are walking the streets, looking for a job, you hear wailing from a house. The crying is so loud that you stop to find out the cause. You discover that a young Jewish woman has died giving birth to a child. Her husband and the newborn infant are left alone. No one seems to care about what happens to them. This chance meeting causes you to think.

If you decide to stay in Milwaukee, trying to ease people's suffering,
turn to page 54.

If you are shocked that Jews can live in such a community and still have no friends, and you choose to seek a smaller place where people know each other,
turn to page 60.

20

Rosenwald is a genius at running the business. He always has the right articles in stock and makes up the orders quickly. You, on the other hand, have a special talent for dealing with customers. They trust you. They know that, if they ask you to bring a specific item, you will deliver it soon and in good condition.

A network of train tracks is beginning to cover the region around Chicago, and, where there are no railroads, wagons regularly travel the roads. Soon, you get a new idea. "Rosenwald," you exclaim, "what if we gave our customers a printed pad of order forms. When they want something, they can write out the description of the merchandise on the form and deliver it to us with the train porter or the wagon-master. We can pay those people a little bit to deliver the order to us. Then, I can take the order to the customer the next time I am traveling in that direction. What do you think?"

Rosenwald quickly appreciates the potential of your idea. You can cover more ground if you have the orders in advance of delivering them. It's a revolutionary concept.

*If you decide to try to increase your business
by traveling to smaller cities,
turn to page 53.*

*If you suspect that Rosenwald will always
run the business with you working for him,
turn to page 59.*

21

Along the southern shore of Lake Michigan, an industrial area has already developed. Small factories make a variety of goods from the raw materials that arrive on wagons and ships and, increasingly, on trains. As you watch all this movement, you realize that soon railroads will become the main form of transportation for this nation—and you want to be a part of this revolution.

The company you establish will build stations and other large structures of concrete and steel. In your vision of the future, you can see large numbers of people riding trains into major cities, arriving in stations you have helped build and walking to their offices and stores. You know that it will be many years, perhaps decades, before this vision becomes reality, but you also know that the people who recognize where history is headed can often help direct its course.

After a number of years trying to make this business a success, you are not sure it really will work. Perhaps you were too far ahead of your time. Yes, you are able to make a living for yourself and your family—but just barely.

If you decide that you have made the right move but just need more time,
turn to page 49.

If you decide to close the business and try something else,
turn to page 50.

22

Working for the Straus family is uninteresting and pays little. Lazarus's sons will always be given the top jobs in this family business. You are right to begin looking elsewhere.

One dusty, hot summer afternoon, a traveler on horseback stops at the Straus store in Talbottom. He is on his way from Mobile, Alabama, to Savannah, Georgia. The Strauses extend hospitality to this weary traveler. After dinner, he tells you about the Mobile Musical Association, led by Sigmund Schlesinger, a gifted Jewish composer, who left Germany and ended up in Alabama. What a change! His songs and choirs are becoming famous throughout the region.

You have not sung for a long time, but you love music, and Schlesinger's reputation is just the motivation you need to move away from Talbottom. You thank the Strauses for all they have done for you and move to Mobile. There, you become a singer in Schlesinger's choir and take a day job as a bookkeeper in a local business. Meanwhile, you keep your eyes open for better opportunities. Two letters come to your attention: One letter from Little Rock, Arkansas, asks the president of the congregation in Mobile if he knows anyone who would come to serve as "rabbi" of their temple. The other letter, addressed to you, is from *Adolph Ochs,* a man in Chattanooga, Tennessee, who is now starting to publish a newspaper. He would like you to consider working for him.

If you decide to go to Little Rock to serve as "rabbi" at the temple, turn to page 65.

If you choose to go to work for Adolph Ochs and his newspaper, turn to page 96.

23

Although you continue working for the Strauses, you are constantly thinking about how you could become a journalist. On December 20, 1860, South Carolina votes to leave the United States. Its citizens believe they are being treated unfairly by the Union and are fearful that slavery, the basis of their society, will be declared illegal. Soon other Southern states also secede, and only a few months later Confederate forces attack the Union army stationed at Fort Sumter in Charleston's harbor.

This is what you have been waiting for: a chance to demonstrate through your reporting skills that you can be a great journalist. Your first thought is to go to Charleston, but you hear that the fighting has ended there. You want to be where there is action, plenty of action.

General Ulysses S. Grant leads his Union army south along the Mississippi River. You can see from the map that he must attack Vicksburg, Mississippi, and that is where you head. And you are right! Grant surrounds the city on three sides with his army; his ships, anchored in the Mississippi below the high bluffs on which the city stands, blockade the city on the west. Suddenly you realize that you are trapped in Vicksburg. You can write all the wonderful words you want, but they will stay with you until the siege lifts.

If you are captured with the Confederate forces and sent to a military prison, turn to page 66.

If you are captured but find a way to make that experience worthwhile, turn to page 97.

24

Even during the few years that you have been in New Orleans, the Jewish community has changed. The older community was composed of French and German Jews and a few even older families of *Sephardic* heritage. They enjoy a particular style of worship, and the synagogue pews have been occupied by the same families for many, many years.

A new group of Jews has begun to arrive, but these German Jews are from Posen. The older Jewish residents of New Orleans think of them as Polish because Posen has been a part of Poland as often as it has been a part of Germany. More importantly, these Jews are different. They pray with a different Hebrew accent and sing different songs. They want a synagogue where they can be comfortable, and that means change, a prospect the older residents do not accept.

A long and bitter argument breaks out between these two groups. As a newcomer yourself, you are caught in the middle. Each group wants you to side with its position. You hate the political feud that is going on, and you can think only of escaping.

*If you decide to leave and head for the
eastern part of Texas,
turn to page 72.*

*If you choose to go even further across the
massive state of Texas,
turn to page 103.*

25

The wagon train crosses the Rockies and then climbs into the Sierra Nevada range of mountains. You find yourself in Virginia City, a silver-mining boom town, not far from the north end of beautiful Lake Tahoe. The entire region is active and lively as eager men and women pour into town, each one hoping to leave with a new fortune.

Adolph Sutro, a self-taught engineer, has invented a new way to separate gold and silver from the rocks and dirt. He also has a new, daring idea. He wants to dig a four-mile-long tunnel under Mount Davidson to the Comstock Lode. The miners will then have fresh air; water will be drained safely out of the mine; and ore will be hauled out more easily.

Most of the new residents of Virginia City are hard-working miners; some are not. A few have come to take advantage of the wealth that the miners dig out of the ground. They cheat at cards, sell "snake-oil" cures that really fix nothing, and even kill luckless miners to steal their riches. The leaders of Virginia City are disgusted by their behavior, but they are not sure what to do about it.

Sutro asks you to come to his office. He tells you that you could do a considerable service to Virginia City by becoming the sheriff. You have never thought about something like that.

If you choose to accept the challenge of becoming the sheriff, turn to page 73.

If, after thanking Sutro for his suggestion, you prefer to seek a more traditional business, turn to page 104.

26

You've never seen a man like this. Wide-brimmed hat, pistol strapped to his belt, fringed leather coat, boots with pointed toes and high heels and metal wheels behind them (later, you learn they are called "spurs")—this must be a real cowboy. He tells you stories of Indians, of nights around the campfire, of driving the cattle from the ranch to the market, of bandits and gamblers, and of danger and hardship.

It's exciting to hear his tales. You can imagine yourself in Arizona, dressed like him, dusty and tired, but having a great adventure. What would your family and friends back in Neustadt think of this? You could send them a picture of you looking like a real American! They would really be impressed.

As you ride toward Arizona on your new horse, you are still rather sore from the rough saddle. A friend offers you two suggestions: You could go to work for the *Goldwater* store. They seem to get along with the Indians, and they can always use new help. Or, perhaps, you could work on a ranch.

If you decide to work for the Goldwater store,
turn to page 79.

If you choose to work on a ranch,
turn to page 110.

27

San Francisco used to be a pleasant small town. Only recently, it changed its name from Yerba Buena, Good Herbs, to that of the Spanish saint. However, the change is more than a name. Now, thousands of people have moved into the city. It is noisy, crowded, dirty. There are many good residents in the city, of course, but there are also some of questionable reputation. The prospect of quick and easy money can attract shady characters.

You think back to Neustadt, the small German town you left less than ten years ago. You remember how much you loved the peace and quiet of that place and how different San Francisco is. That thought helps you make a decision. You cannot live in this city; you must go somewhere where life is more kind and gentle. Asking around, you find that there are several places in California that might be right for you.

You can travel down the coastline, past Los Angeles, all the way to San Diego. Graced by a magnificent harbor, the town has become a haven for whaling and fishing vessels, but not much else goes on.

The other possibility is to go inland to a town like Bakersfield. Only a few hardy people have migrated to the central California desert, and you will certainly find peace there.

*If you decide to go to San Diego,
turn to page 84.*

*If you prefer to go to Bakersfield,
turn to page 116.*

28

Fechheimer makes shirts. Before he opened his factory, women would sew shirts at home for their families. Now, dozens of seamstresses work in a large room, sewing shirt after shirt, hundreds every day. There are three sizes—small, medium, and large—and only two colors—gray and light tan. They cost far less than the shirts that were made at home, and it is easier for most people to buy them than to sew them for themselves.

Fechheimer gives you a job in the office as a clerk. You keep records on how much material was purchased, when it was used, and how much will be needed in the future. This is important work: If the factory runs out of cloth, it can't make any more shirts! The work may be important, but it isn't very exciting. You sit at a big ledger all day and enter numbers. There must be more to life than this!

Turn to page 7.

29

The Seinsheimer Company is also in the clothing business. To make their shirts, trousers, and skirts, they need cotton— cotton from the states south of the Ohio River. You are sent into this region to buy the cotton crops of the various plantations. You travel up and down the Mississippi River, stopping wherever a market offers the kind of cotton Seinsheimer needs. When you make a purchase, you send a telegraph message to the home office in Cincinnati, telling them to expect a shipment and asking them to send you money to pay for the cotton.

There are others who engage in the same business. Some of them are honest, as you are; others are not. You avoid them as much as you can because you realize that your future depends on people being able to trust your word. If the growers have no confidence in you, they will not sell you the cotton, or they will sell it to you at a higher price. You must have an absolutely honest reputation. The *crown of a good name* is your most cherished possession.

As you come to love the South, you think you might like to settle there permanently. One town in particular, Holly Springs, Mississippi, reminds you of the area of Germany where you grew up.

On the other hand, you are also aware of growing tensions between the North and the South. Talk of war is in the air, and you might want to hold off making any commitments until you see what is going to happen.

If you decide to move to Holly Springs, turn to page 56.

If you choose to continue in your present job and wait to see what happens, turn to page 63.

30

You are assigned to Company H of the Eighth Georgia Infantry. With the rest of your friends, you march, practice shooting, train—and wait. Many of the soldiers wish for a battle; they look forward to the glory of victory. You are not so sure, but you keep your doubts to yourself.

When the call comes, your regiment marches north to Virginia. Just outside Manassas, one great battle already has been fought. Now, armies are gathering for a second. Your comrades honor you by electing you to carry the regimental colors, the flag that must always lead the attack. Some honor! you think to yourself, but you keep quiet.

You dash forward during the infantry charge. Smoke and noise, the screams of falling men, and the confusion of battle are all around you. You feel a musket ball pass through your leg, but it's only a flesh wound, and you continue. When the battle is over, you limp back to your tent, expecting your wound to heal. But it doesn't. An ugly infection almost leads to the loss of your leg.

After the war, you return home. But it's not the same. Soldiers and politicians from the North are in charge. They call it Reconstruction, but they seem to be changing everything only for the worse. You cannot stay; this is no longer the South that you had grown to love. The new frontier of America is still California, and that is where you will head.

If you decide to take a ship around South America,
turn to page 67.

If you choose to travel overland,
turn to page 98.

31

As much as you love your friends, you can't agree with their ideas. You know that slavery is wrong. Sure, the Bible tells us that Abraham and other ancient Jews had slaves. But that was thousands of years ago. It's incredible to you that now someone would have the right to own another person, to sell one person away from his or her family, or to beat or chain someone because of poor work. It's just wrong!

You leave Georgia and travel west. In Kansas, you hear tales of August Bondi, a Jew who rides with John Brown. You track down their party in Osawatomie and join up. With this band of rugged horsemen, you ride through the rolling Kansas prairie, doing everything you can to prevent Kansas from becoming a slave state. Usually, you and your companions ride into a town, tie your horses outside the saloon, and speak to everyone you can find. Some are easy to convince; others, especially those who have migrated to Kansas from the South, are not. At other times, you are not so peaceful; on night raids, you even set fire to the barns of leaders of the proslavery group.

Brown becomes more of a fanatic. You hear stories that he even killed five men a few years ago. You become disenchanted with this unusual man. Then he leaves for Canada. Just as well! You were not thrilled to be involved in the violence he preached. Kansas had no attraction for you, other than Brown, Bondi, and their mission. You decide to leave, too.

If you decide to head west on the trails to Utah,
turn to page 71.

If you prefer to go north into Nebraska,
turn to page 102.

32

When you arrive in Santa Fe, it is almost as if you had entered another foreign country. You came to the United States speaking German. Now, you have learned English. But here you must use Spanish! You listen to the odd sounds of the language as you walk down the street, until . . . until you hear a very different sound, someone speaking *Yiddish*. A *landsman*! He is Solomon Jacob Spiegelberg, born in Prussia, now living in New Mexico. "Call me S.J. Everyone does. Come on! You look as if you could use a good meal. Let's find you some food and a bed."

S.J. and his five brothers have bought land, opened mines, and operate a number of stores. They ask you what you can do. You tell them that you'll take almost any job but that, if you had your choice, you'd love to find something that involved art. "I like to draw. I'm a good engraver."

What a coincidence! Because there is no bank in New Mexico, each merchant issues his own money. The Spiegelbergs are so well known and trusted that their bank notes are considered especially valuable. "We need a new one," the brothers tell you. "We need a bill for doce y medio centavos, 'twelve and one-half cents,' payable on the Spiegelberg Hermanos Bank. Can you do that?" You quickly agree and produce a fine-looking bill. The Spiegelbergs are happy and give you other jobs to do in their business.

*If you decide to take over the freight line
that brings merchandise for their stores,
turn to page 77.*

*If you choose to move away from town and
trade with the Indians,
turn to page 108.*

33

You join a mule train that leaves St. Joseph, Missouri. It is led by *Colonel John C. Fremont,* a famous soldier and explorer. The most interesting person in the group is Solomon Nunes Carvalho, a *Sephardic* Jew who is a specialist in daguerreotype photography. Fremont has asked Carvalho to record western scenes, sights that most Americans have never seen. It is Fremont's dream that Americans will become so excited by these pictures that they will move west and settle in this new region.

You are hired to be Carvalho's assistant. To make a single image may take two or three hours, after carrying heavy equipment from the mules to the place where Carvalho will set up his camera. It's hard work, but you learn a great deal. You see the most beautiful scenery you could ever imagine.

The weather becomes worse, and some of the members of the party become so ill that they die. Carvalho himself survives only because the Mormons who live in Parowan, Utah, nurse him back to health. His adventure with Fremont is over, and you must find something new to do.

If you choose to travel south to seek your fortune in the new city of Denver, turn to page 78.

If you decide to stay in the high country because you love the mountains, turn to page 109.

34

Your decision is easy when you hear that gold has been discovered up the coast near Eureka. You quickly make your way to that boom town. To your immense surprise, you find a small Jewish community, complete with a tiny synagogue and a *bet olam,* a cemetery.

However, it's not among the Jews that you find your fortune. You frequent the saloons, where you learn to handle a deck of cards, not always honestly. It's during one of the card games, as your stack of chips and money begins to rise before you, that one of the other players accuses you of cheating. He pulls out a gun and fires at you point-blank. As you fall to the floor, you wonder if you will soon be lying in the *bet olam.*

That is not quite to be. You are seriously wounded but recover. Your quest for gold has not panned out, and you wonder whether or not you should bet your future on this region.

If you choose to return to the safety of San Francisco,
turn to page 85.

If you decide to continue northward to seek more frontier adventures,
turn to page 117.

35

San Francisco is an exciting, bustling city. Raised in a small town, you've never known a place that was more interesting than this big city. It's here that you feel you have to stay and make your future.

On *Shabbat* morning, you ask someone on the street, "Where is the synagogue?" He doesn't seem to understand you. Then you get an idea. You want to find a place where Jewish people go to pray. "Oh," he replies. "I understand. You want Temple Emanu-El. I have heard that it is the most beautiful building in all of San Francisco."

When you enter Temple Emanu-El's sanctuary, you realize that the man was right: It is beautiful. You hear familiar sounds of spoken German. The worshipers sit quietly, responding only when they are told to do so, and the rabbi gives a fine, intelligent sermon. In the back corner of the temple, however, a small group of people—they look somehow different—huddle, talking in low voices. You can tell they are not happy. "We are from Poland. These kinds of services are not for us. We don't speak German, and they pronounce Hebrew with a different accent. We want our own *minhag.*"

If you decide to leave San Francisco because of the conflict between the Jewish groups, turn to page 86.

If you choose to stay in San Francisco and join the congregation started by the Polish Jews, turn to page 118.

36

You secure a job with the American Fur Company, a large business that sends its representatives north from Michigan into Canada. Every summer, as the river ice thaws, you and your Indian guides leave Mackinac and head north. You do not return until late fall. While you are in the north woods, you live like an Indian, sleeping outside, eating their food, learning their language. When you come to a settlement, you trade the goods that you have brought from Michigan for the furs that the Indians have trapped. The Crees come to respect you so much that they call you Bosh-bish-gay-bish-gensen, a name in their language that means "firecracker."

After several years of traveling and trading, you have amassed quite a bit of money. It's time, you say to yourself, to settle down, start a family, and stop being such a nomad. However, you cannot accomplish this goal in Mackinac. You must move to a new location.

If you decide that the new mining country in the Upper Peninsula of Michigan and Minnesota shows great promise, turn to page 18.

If you choose to go to a city where there are many German Jews like yourself, turn to page 19.

37

Only a few hundred Jews live in Chicago, but the community grows every day. They have formed a synagogue, *Anshe Ma'ariv,* which holds services daily in the back room of Rosenfeld and Rosenberg's store. People engage in all sorts of business: groceries, plumbing, carpentery, peddling. The needs of this frontier city are so vast that almost anyone who wants to work hard can do very well.

You find your place in this whirlwind of a city by carrying a pack of dry goods—a selection of just about anything other than food that you can lift onto your back. People who live a few miles outside the city are glad to have you visit because they have no stores of their own. They especially appreciate the news and gossip you bring from Chicago.

After one such trip, while having dinner at the boarding house where you live, you turn to a friend, Samuel Rosenwald, who works as a clerk at Hammerslough's clothing store, and give him a new idea. "What if people let me know in advance what they want to buy? Then, I could carry only those preordered items. It would be a real service to them and very efficient for me. I could just deliver their goods and move along."

You also come up with another thought. More railroad traffic arrives in Chicago every day. "I bet there is a need for stations for these trains. Maybe I could learn how to build them."

If you decide to go into business with Rosenwald, who likes your idea, turn to page 20.

If you choose to build railroad train stations, turn to page 21.

38

The news is everywhere. Gold and silver have been discovered in California, Colorado, Alaska—all throughout the West. Boats leave every day for San Francisco. You cannot resist. You, too, want to be part of this excitement and seek your fortune on the frontier of America.

The boat you take sails around the southern tip of South America. Most of the time, the weather is awful, and you are fearfully seasick. It is only when you pass Mexico that the seas become calm, and you feel somewhat better. You hope that the streets are really paved with gold because you've suffered enough; the trip had better be worth it!

As you swing in your hammock at night, looking up at the millions of stars in the heavens, you feel like Jacob in the Bible: "Surely God is in this place. . . ." [Genesis 28:16] With God's presence, your trip will certainly succeed.

Your ship docks in San Francisco, and you finally set foot on dry land. It has been a long voyage, and you are thrilled to have arrived safely. You meet two men, each of whom has an idea of what you ought to do: One man tells you about the Arizona Territory; you are fascinated by his tales. The other man offers to show you around the city.

If you consider going to the Arizona Territory,
turn to page 26.

If you decide to walk around and see the city of San Francisco,
turn to page 27.

39

You cross the Isthmus of Panama on foot, swatting huge mosquitoes and hoping that you will not catch some deadly sickness. Some people on the trip take ill, and some even die, but you are lucky. On the Pacific side, you board another ship, up the coast and into San Francisco harbor.

The wharf area around the docks is rough. Rowdy sailors often get into fights, sometimes pulling out knives or guns. You observe a brawl as you set foot off the boat. A monstrously huge man is bearing down on a much smaller one with a shining dagger raised to strike. Suddenly, the smaller man points a pistol at his attacker and pulls the trigger. The assailant staggers, then sinks to the ground in a pool of his own blood.

The police take your name as a witness, but you think nothing more of the incident until you are summoned to testify in court. You ask to be excused because the date of the trial has been set for *Yom Kippur.* You explain to the judge that no Jew can testify in court on such a holy day. He is not sympathetic and orders you locked up for contempt. Only after the holy day, when you can give your evidence, are you released. You wonder if you should stay in a city that is so intolerant of Jews. Or, perhaps, this was just an isolated incident.

If you choose to leave San Francisco, turn to page 34.

If you decide to give the city a second chance, turn to page 35.

40

Cleveland is still a small city on the Cuyahoga River. The water is so clear you can see fish swimming upstream. "What a lovely place! I could easily settle here and spend the rest of my life in such a city. It even reminds me of Neustadt, although I do miss the mountains." Later, you travel just east of the city and discover a section the people are beginning to call "The Heights." While the hills there are not as high as those of Neustadt, they're better than nothing. If you ever move out of the city itself, that's where you'll live.

Many Jews in Cleveland have recently come from Germany. Like you, they are trying to decide where in America they want to live, what jobs they want to take, and what they want to do with the rest of their lives. Many of them are young and single. There are clubs for young Jewish men and separate clubs for young Jewish women. Sometimes they go on picnics together, hold dances, and, in the spring, there is the famous Strawberry Festival. The women make desserts with strawberries, and the men buy them. When you buy a dessert, the woman who made it becomes your partner for the rest of the party.

If you decide you might stay in Cleveland for the rest of your life because it is a city with a great future,
turn to page 15.

If you decide to move to a beautiful little country town called Circleville, about which you have been told and which resembles the farm town of Neustadt from which you came,
turn to page 17.

41

Rabbi Wise may have lost the fight on the pulpit, but, when he speaks, his voice convinces you that he will change the Jewish world. Perhaps it's his commitment, almost as if he were on a mission.

Wise is elected the rabbi of B'nai Yeshurun, a liberal congregation in Cincinnati, Ohio. You read reports of his installation service in *Isaac Leeser*'s newspaper, *The Occident*. Quite an event!—congregation members holding Torahs in a parade from Wise's home to the temple; a three-hour service with a sermon by Wise on his vision for a liberal Jewish future in America; an installation attended by non-Jews; and a front-page report of the events in the Cincinnati newspaper, treatment usually afforded only to a major story. Perhaps it was.

All this convinces you to go to Cincinnati, where your future will somehow be connected to this small, but powerful, rabbi. You secure a letter of introduction from some of the most prominent people in the congregation in Albany. This letter will help you meet the leading Jews of Cincinnati and find work. Making your way back through New York City, then west through the Cumberland Gap by horse-drawn wagon, and down the Ohio River on a flat-bottom boat, you reach Cincinnati from Albany. The letter of introduction works, and you are soon offered two different types of employment: a position in the Fechheimer shirt factory and a job, buying and selling on the road, with the Seinsheimer Company.

If you decide to accept the position in the Fechheimer shirt factory, turn to page 28.

*If you choose to take the job with the
Seinsheimer Company,
turn to page 29.*

Isaac Mayer Wise

Isaac Leeser

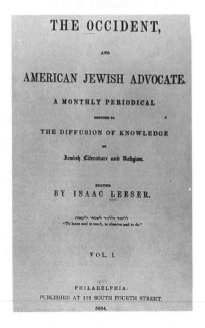

THE OCCIDENT,

AND

AMERICAN JEWISH ADVOCATE.

A MONTHLY PERIODICAL

DEVOTED TO

THE DIFFUSION OF KNOWLEDGE

ON

Jewish Literature and Religion.

EDITED

BY ISAAC LEESER.

ללמד וללמוד לשמור ולעשות
"To learn and to teach, to observe and to do."

VOL. I.

PHILADELPHIA:
PUBLISHED AT 118 SOUTH FOURTH STREET.
5604.

43

"You see," a woman tells you, "New Orleans has a terrible problem. Every few years, there is an epidemic of disease. Cholera, yellow fever, and malaria sweep through the population, and there is not much we can do about it. The illnesses attack everyone, rich and poor, Jew and non-Jew. We all suffer. The ones who suffer most are the children whose parents die. We have decided to open an orphan asylum where they can live in safety and receive schooling and religious instruction. We shall also try to find families where we can place these unfortunates."

You agree to become a teacher in the new orphan asylum, and soon you have become very attached to the children who live there. Their lives have been made bitter by the tragic deaths of their parents; you have the chance to bring them some light and warmth.

The managers of the home, however, are more successful than they expected. Within a few years, the epidemic is gone, and all the children have been adopted into new homes. Some were sent as far away as Chicago, where they had distant relatives; others remain in New Orleans. As for you, it is time to find another job.

If you decide to stay in New Orleans,
turn to page 24.

If you decide to seek more adventure before
settling down,
turn to page 25.

44

Shortly after you arrive in New Orleans, the argument over slavery becomes very heated. Everyday there are marches in favor of it. People who dare to speak against this system are beaten and run out of town. On *Shabbat* morning, you hear a sermon by *Rabbi James K. Gutheim,* a very distinguished Jewish leader, who tells his congregations, "It is not fitting from this pulpit to pursue the political questions of the day."

When his sermon is over, long before the service has been completed, you leave the synagogue. You cannot believe he avoided the moral issue of whether slavery is good or evil. Never had you expected to hear a rabbi fail to speak against a system that treats human beings so brutally. "Weren't we slaves in Egypt ourselves? We didn't like that experience. Why would we think it is acceptable for anyone else?" You suppose that Rabbi Gutheim has been in the South too long; he has become just like his neighbors. Your respect for rabbis is sadly diminished as you think about what he said.

Clearly, you cannot stay in New Orleans. If you feel this way about slavery, this is not the place for you. Some people tell you about a wonderful and exciting territory called New Mexico. You also hear about an expedition that will explore the northern part of the Rocky Mountains.

If you choose to go to New Mexico,
turn to page 32.

If you decide to explore the northern part of
the Rockies,
turn to page 33.

45

The peddler, you discover, is the only source of outside news for people isolated in small towns. When you arrive, people listen eagerly to your tales of business dealings, wars, and politics. They especially want to know about the interesting people you have met or heard about. You become a human newspaper. It's a job you enjoy. Sometimes you catch yourself making the stories sound even better than they really are!

You realize that it would be helpful to these folks if there were a national newspaper you could bring to them. You hear that *Julius and Adolph Ochs* of Chattanooga, Tennessee, are interested in starting a newspaper, but nothing has yet come of their plans. However, you write to them, telling of your interest in their project.

You also learn that Rabbi Isaac Mayer Wise of Cincinnati, Ohio, has begun a paper called *The American Israelite*. He also publishes a German-language paper called *Die Deborah*. You communicate with Rabbi Wise, asking if he would be interested in having you submit stories and also distribute his papers to news-hungry Jews as you make your rounds. He writes back with keen enthusiasm, and you now have a second job.

If you find your first job, with the Strauses, uninteresting, and you don't like working for other people,
turn to page 22.

If you decide to pursue a career in journalism, having realized that you love writing stories,
turn to page 23.

46

Business does not go well for the Strauses and their neighbors. You hear talk in town about banks in the North that will not lend money to the South, about railroads that have been built from the North to the Midwest, not to the South, about unfair business practices and attacks on the system of slaveholding—all of which have made it difficult to succeed in business in Talbottom and in other towns and cities in the South.

By 1857, conditions are even worse; business failures grow; the nation is in an economic depression, but the South is hit hardest. In many states there is talk about leaving the Union and beginning a new country. South Carolina secedes in 1860; other states soon follow. War breaks out in April 1861, when Confederate troops attack the Union garrison at Fort Sumter, an island in the harbor of Charleston, South Carolina.

You have been happy in Talbottom. The people who live there have been your friends. If they believe so strongly in the Southern cause, perhaps you ought to join their struggle. Maybe this is the only way to assure fair treatment for the South.

However, although you love your neighbors, you cannot bring yourself to fight for the slave system. Perhaps you should leave this region.

*If you choose to support the Southern cause,
turn to page 30.*

*If you decide to leave the South,
turn to page 31.*

47

Along the Cuyahoga River, there are many factories. Some make wagons; others fashion barrels. Blacksmiths hammer out tools and horseshoes. Masons cut stone for the new buildings that seem to sprout up every day. Carpenters, potters, shoemakers, tailors—Cleveland seems to have a job for everyone. One evening you notice that the men who work in these factories and those who work on their own have one thing in common: Before they leave their workplaces, they sit down for a few minutes and take out a cigar. Everyone of them. They light their cigars, puff for a while, and talk with one another. Then each one walks home, still smoking the cigar. What an interesting custom!

To see where this social tradition leads you, turn to page 123.

48

You rent a piece of property in "The Heights" that has a beautiful grove of maple trees and a large barn. The owner shows you how to tap the trees in the spring so that the sap will flow into buckets. From the sap you can make maple syrup. In the barn there is plenty of room for you to raise animals. The eagle is the national bird, but no one eats eagles. Instead, you raise turkeys, the bird that Benjamin Franklin wanted to have as the national bird.

Unfortunately for you, nobody told you that turkeys are very difficult to raise. They get sick, and most of them die. And, after a rather warm winter, the sap only drips slowly out of the trees—not enough to make even a few gallons of syrup. You think: After all those centuries when anti-Semites prohibited Jews from owning land in Europe, I guess we forgot how to be farmers. You return to Cleveland and choose a new path.

If you choose to open a small store, turn to page 69.

If you decide to spend your life helping other immigrants, turn to page 100.

49

One of the problems you have had is securing enough steel to reinforce the concrete of your structures. There are no steel mills in the Chicago area; most of this material is made around Pittsburgh, Pennsylvania.

You take the train to Pittsburgh. One of your friends has given you a letter of introduction to a prominent attorney there, and he, in turn, helps you meet people in the steel-supply business. You talk to a number of companies and eventually find one led by men with whom you feel comfortable. As you continue working out the details of the business deal, you become friends with these men and their families. That's important because you will have to work with them when you are back in Chicago and they are still in Pittsburgh. If you have people you like and trust, you can have more confidence in the outcome of your dealings.

Your business prospers, and you find that you have more than enough money to live on. You must now decide how to invest the savings that you have accumulated.

If you decide that the future of the steel industry is in East Chicago, turn to page 93.

If you choose to invest your money in land, turn to page 121.

50

Over the years, you have exchanged mail with a cousin who lives in Bluefield, West Virginia. She writes you that the coal mines are booming in this region, and there are excellent opportunities for someone to open a small store. At the present time, she writes, there is only one store. It is owned by the mining company, and all the miners and their families must shop there. The prices are so high that they spend more than they earn. They end up owing the store money at the end of each month and must work the next month just to pay off that debt. It's a form of slavery, she tells you.

With her encouragement, you move to Bluefield and open a general store. The mine owners try to shut you down. One evening, some thugs throw a burning torch into your store, but you are lucky; you are working late and are able to put out the fire before it does much damage. From that night on, you and your clerks take turns sitting in the darkened store with a shotgun. No one will take this opportunity away from you!

If you decide to do something to change the living conditions of these people, turn to page 94.

If you are convinced that you cannot change the system, turn to page 122.

51

When you are in Columbus for *Rosh Hashanah,* you visit the campus of Ohio State University. It's overwhelming; there must be several thousand students, and that scares you. You would never be able to find your way among so many people. There's a smaller school east of Circleville—Marietta College in Marietta, Ohio—and that's where you go. The teachers pay attention to you and help you when there are words and ideas you have trouble understanding. Their care persuades you to become a teacher. You study pedagogy and, in four years, graduate as an educator.

It's possible, you think, for you to teach young children. But the teachers who influenced you most were those who taught you as an adult. Isn't there some kind of teaching where the students would not be children?

One possibility is to enroll in Rabbi Isaac Mayer Wise's new rabbinical school, the Hebrew Union College, in Cincinnati. Rabbis are teachers, and that might be just right for you. On the other hand, you wonder if you should become a college teacher like those you have come to admire.

If you choose to enroll in the Hebrew Union College to become a rabbi,
turn to page 70.

If you prefer to become a college teacher,
turn to page 101.

52

More and more people are coming across the Appalachian Mountains into the Ohio River valley. Each one of these people will need to buy things—things to build their houses, things to run their farms and businesses, things to eat, and things to wear. Surely, almost any business you decide to open will succeed. The question is what type of business.

Some of your friends urge you to open a hardware store. They show you a place next to the blacksmith's shop, which, they tell you, would be ideal for such a business. "Everybody will need pots and pans, nails and tools. The blacksmith can make many of these things on his anvil, and you can sell them in partnership with him. There's no way you can fail."

On the other hand, you are reminded that a family can survive with one pot, but everyone needs clothing. Children, especially, need new clothes as they grow. What they can wear one year won't fit the next. A clothing store is very likely to make you a success.

*If you decide that a hardware store would be
a good idea,
turn to page 74.*

*If you prefer to own a clothing shop,
turn to page 105.*

53

You can only cover so much territory yourself, and America is such a huge country. Even the area within a hundred miles of Chicago is too much for you to manage personally. There must be a better way.

As you talk with a shopkeeper in Springfield, Illinois, you have a thought. "I can't come down here regularly, but you live here. If you would work for us, visiting all the small towns and farmers in the vicinity, you could collect their orders and send them to us or bring them up on the train. We could fill the orders quickly, and you could deliver the goods. Of course, we would pay you a percentage of whatever sales you make."

That's the solution, you say to yourself. I will get representatives for our company from the smaller towns and cities. Each can have an assigned territory. Then, I won't have to travel so much, and we can cover a much larger area.

Rosenwald thinks the idea is outstanding, and the two of you recruit representatives throughout the Midwest. The business grows very quickly as you provide a necessary and convenient service for many families.

If, as you reach your own middle age, you decide to retire and do something else, turn to page 91.

If you choose to continue with Rosenwald, turn to page 119.

You turn to other people on the street, asking: "Is there a Jewish funeral home here? How will the poor woman be buried?" No one seems to know the answer. When you ask at the synagogue, you are told there is a Jewish cemetery west of the city but no Jewish funeral home. "We use a non-Jewish undertaker and do the best we can," a leader of the community says.

Now, you know what you must do. You open a strictly *kosher* Jewish funeral home in the middle of the area where most of the Jews live, six or seven blocks west of the lakefront. "The poor woman who died and others like her may not have had any friends or family, but at least I shall provide a proper funeral and a *minyan* of mourners. To make sure that a Jew is laid to rest in the *bet olam,* in the cemetery, is the greatest *mitzvah* I can do."

As the years pass, you become a leader of the Jewish community in Milwaukee. You now have the leisure time to devote to communal affairs, even though you continue in business.

*If you decide to spend your spare time
helping new immigrants,
turn to page 88.*

*If you prefer to focus your activities on your
synagogue,
turn to page 114.*

55

You send a letter to your family in Neustadt. "There are lots of jobs here in Virginia, Minnesota. If you can send some of my cousins to live here, I think they will have a fine opportunity. I am enclosing some money to pay for their tickets. Please hurry. I don't know how long I can keep up this pace; I am exhausted and sleep only three or four hours each night."

The letter takes almost four months to reach Neustadt, but the family is overjoyed to hear from you. They are pleased that you have been so successful and send four of your cousins, two men and two women, all teenagers, to help you. It takes another four months or so before they arrive. They cannot speak English, and they seem lost in this new culture. But you reassure them that you once started out as they did; soon, they, too, will be Americans.

Your idea was correct. With their help in the kitchen, in the store, in the saloon, in the boarding house, the business runs smoothly. You can even take a day off once in a while. Other young German Jews come to join you; soon you have enough for a *minyan* every morning before work. What a turn of events! you think. Here we are in northern Minnesota, far from a large Jewish community, and still we can pray like other Jews, keep a part of our tradition alive, even try to keep some of the *kosher* food laws. It won't be long before we can build our own *shul.*

Turn to page 82.

56

The streets of Holly Springs are lined with well-kept wooden houses, each one painted a different pastel color. The one main street has eight or ten stores on each side, and there is even talk of installing a wooden sidewalk so shoppers will not have to walk in the mud on rainy days. Of course, there are other sections of town—sections where black slaves live. These sections are very different. Conditions in these areas are far worse than anywhere you have ever lived. But, for the white residents of the town, it is indeed a pleasant place to live.

You open a business as a cotton factor, a person who buys bales of cotton from plantations and resells them to traders, people who have come down from northern factories to find the raw materials for clothing and other goods. As your business increases, you also sell other agricultural products: some rice, some corn, some vegetables.

Everything seems to be going well until the Civil War begins. The invading Army of the Tennessee under General Grant cuts off many of the supplies the region needs. It becomes harder and harder to conduct business, making life more difficult than it was before the war. People become irritated, frustrated, angry, and you begin to hear rumors that the hardships of life are really the fault of the few Jews who live in the area.

If, despite being hurt by these rumors, you decide to remain in Holly Springs, turn to page 80.

If you are furious because of the anti-Semitic comments and choose to leave, turn to page 111.

57

You are not the only young German Jew who peddles through the countryside, selling Fechheimer shirts. Mr. Fechheimer has made a practice of encouraging young people to come to Cincinnati and work in his factory for a year or two. When they learn enough English to manage away from the city, he gives them a backpack of shirts on credit and sends them out on a particular route. After they have successfully sold their merchandise, he lends them a horse and wagon, refilled with shirts and trousers. With this equipment, they can travel farther from Cincinnati, selling to people who cannot be visited by foot peddlers.

Over time, you graduate to this second level of peddling. Your territory is northeast of Indianapolis, Indiana, and you do very well. As the years pass, however, you begin to wonder: Shouldn't I really settle down? Maybe I should find a town where I can live permanently, raise a family, and enjoy a more relaxed and stable life.

One of the towns you have been visiting while peddling your goods is Marion, a small farming town, which seems to have considerable possibility for growth.

From one of the daily newspapers you have read as your horse plods along the dirt roads of Indiana you have learned about a new wave of immigration. Scandinavians—people from Norway and Sweden, Finland and Denmark—are arriving in America in large numbers, and many of them are going out to a new territory, the Dakotas. "What an opportunity!" you shout aloud. "I could go out there, help them get settled, and also make a fortune."

If you choose to settle in Marion, Indiana,
turn to page 75.

58

If you choose to move out to the Dakota Territories,

turn to page 106.

59

You realize that the Rosenwald family will always own this business. As large as it may become, their children and grandchildren will be in the top positions; your future is limited.

One *Shabbat* morning a few weeks after *Simchat Torah,* as you sit in the pews of *Anshe Ma'ariv,* you are surprised to hear some words of advice coming from the Torah scroll. "You shall spread out to the west. . . ." [Genesis 28:14], the reader chants. You had just read in the newspaper that *Horace Greeley* had advised young people: "If you have . . . no prospect opened to you . . . , turn your face to the great West, and there build up a home and fortune."

Greeley and the Torah! That the two agree cannot be a coincidence. You are sure that this is the path you must follow. The problem is to decide exactly where to go.

If you choose to head for St. Louis, Missouri, turn to page 92.

If you decide to be even more daring and strike out for St. Joseph, Missouri, the starting place for the trails into the Great Plains,
turn to page 120.

60

Seventy miles west of Milwaukee is the small city of Madison. It is the state capital and home of the University of Wisconsin. If you walk north five minutes from the state capital building, you are on the shores of Lake Mendota. Madison is a beautiful place to live.

You move to Madison. A few blocks from the center of the city, the small Jewish community has already built a handsome, tan stone synagogue. There is no rabbi, but the members take turns leading the services. As you enter its doors on your first *Shabbat* morning in Madison, you notice a name over the door: Sha'arei Shamayim, Congregation Gates of Heaven.

After a few months, one of the community leaders asks if you would be interested in becoming a paid employee of the congregation.

If you decide to accept the offer to be a paid employee of Sha'arei Shamayim,
turn to page 89.

If, on the other hand, you would prefer to study law,
turn to page 115.

61

Others can see the potential for profit in the various enterprises you have established, and you sell your business easily. Soon, you are on your way to the new territorial capital city, St. Paul.

Only a little over a hundred Jews live in St. Paul when you arrive; any newcomer is an important addition to their community. They have plans to start a burial committee, purchase a cemetery, and found a synagogue. Some even talk of a mutual assistance society, a kind of insurance plan through which you could help one another during times of illness, death, and need. Right now, plans can wait. You must find a job.

You begin working in a brewery, making the strong beer that the German and Bohemian workers love. Because of your hard work and intelligence, you are soon promoted to foreman. When the owner of the brewery dies from influenza, you arrange to purchase the business from his widow. She is glad to sell a business she could not run by herself, and you are overjoyed to be your own boss. As time passes, you consider your next move.

Business has been good, but you are concerned that the supply of grain that you need for brewing is uncertain. You can, however, think about another career. The business now supports you nicely; you do not have to worry about money. Perhaps you ought to do something to contribute to the community that has given so much to you.

If you decide to stay in the brewery business by guaranteeing the necessary grain supply, turn to page 87.

62

If you choose to undertake a new career that will result in your contributing substantially to the community,

turn to page 113.

63

You travel frequently up and down the Ohio and Mississippi rivers, searching for plantations with cotton to sell. Year after year, you visit growers who have now become friends. When you call upon them, it is almost as though you were coming to meet members of your family.

During one trip, you disembark from the paddle wheeler north of Vicksburg. Usually, a horse and buggy from the plantation meet you there, but this time is different. Four rough-looking men with guns confront you, tie you up, and throw you into a wagon. "This Jew ought to be worth a lot of money to someone," one of them says, and they send a ransom note to Vicksburg.

The leaders of that city's small Jewish community have never had to think about something like this. When they meet, however, one of them speaks: "In Europe where we all came from, there was an obligation, a *mitzvah,* for Jews always to secure the release of fellow Jews. It is called *pidyon shevuyim,* 'ransoming the captives.' We have no choice." The ransom money is quickly collected, and you are are rescued from the bandits who had captured you.

If, impressed by the generosity of the Jews of Vicksburg, you decide to stay in that city, turn to page 81.

If, despite your gratitude, you decide you cannot stay there, turn to page 112.

64

You meet with Rabbi Wise at his home one *Shabbat* afternoon and explain to him your interest in becoming a rabbi. He smiles and tells you that this is a wonderful idea. "There's only one problem. There is no school in America where you can fulfill your ambition. I tried to start the Zion Collegiate Academy a few years ago, but too few people supported the school. If you want to become a rabbi, you'll have to study in Germany.

"But I've got another idea," Rabbi Wise continues. "If you really want to help people, you could become a doctor. The University of Cincinnati has opened an excellent medical school. Helping physically ill people is certainly as important as helping spiritually needy ones. Besides, no one says that you have to be a rabbi to make a contribution to Jewish life; as a lay person, you can also have great influence."

Rabbi Wise is right. You are not prepared to return to Germany, and you do want to help people. So, you enroll in medical school and study very hard. As you approach graduation, you decide you want to become an orthopedic surgeon, repairing broken bones and joints.

One of your professors reminds you that the best training for doctors is also in Germany. He urges you to go back for a year or two, pursue advanced studies, and then bring that learning and skill back to Cincinnati.

If you decide to return to Germany for a short time to advance your medical studies, turn to page 76.

If you choose to practice medicine immediately, not desiring to return to Europe, turn to page 107.

65

The temple in Little Rock has just been founded, and its board cannot afford to hire an ordained rabbi. You think you can perform most rabbinic tasks—lead services, marry, bury, teach children—so you send a letter offering your services. It is not long before you learn that you would be welcome in that city.

Bidding goodbye to Schlesinger and thanking him for all he has taught you about Jewish music and prayer, you make the move. It turns out to be a position for which you are ideally suited. The congregation grows to love you, and you are extremely happy there.

Over the years, you wonder: Perhaps God had a purpose for me all along. Perhaps it was meant for me to end up here in the middle of America, helping keep Judaism alive among good and generous people. The idea certainly makes sense to me.

END

DER PEDLER

66

The siege of Vicksburg is horrible. Cannon fire from the Union ships falls without distinguishing between civilians and soldiers; women, children, and men; white and black. You see more injury and death than you could have ever imagined; misery is all about you.

Finally, the military commander of Vicksburg concedes defeat and surrenders. The Union soldiers enter the city and begin to march its defenders off to military prisons. They take you, too, and it does absolutely no good that you shout, "I am not a soldier; I am a journalist; you have the wrong person." No one listens. You are just another "Johnny Reb," and the victorious men in blue couldn't care less about your pleas.

You spend the rest of the war years behind the stockade, cooped up with other Confederate soldiers. Many die of disease, but you are lucky. You survive.

After the war, you are released. But where to go? What to do? Then, you think to yourself: I guess it's no different from when I got off the boat from Germany. Then I had nothing; now I have nothing. Then I made a pretty good life for myself; now I can do the same. And so you set off, determined to rebuild your life.

Turn to page 33.

67

You return to Savannah and board the first available ship. It takes weeks and weeks to reach California. Part of that time you are terribly seasick. The waves and weather around Cape Horn are especially vicious. Finally, you enter the harbor of San Francisco and walk down the gangplank.

The first news you hear is that there is a plague in the city. Many are seriously ill, and quite a number have died. You have just been healed of a life-threatening infection, and the last place you want to be is among sick people. You turn around and reboard the ship; it sails up the California coast, eventually arriving in Vancouver, British Columbia.

When you disembark at this western Canadian town, you notice that the air is crystal-clear, and a sense of excitement and energy is in the wind. The scenery is beautiful, and something else strikes you: the trees. There are tall pine trees everywhere. They're awesome to look at, but you see something else: their potential as lumber. The West in both Canada and the United States will be growing rapidly; there will be an immense demand for wood building products. The lumber business must be a surefire success.

You open a sawmill on the outskirts of Vancouver, using your military pay to help you get started. As you think back on it, the Civil War was not glorious but awful; but, at least, it helped you fashion a new life.

END

68

Your cigar factory is a huge success. After a number of years, you own several factories, each one making a different style of cigar. You have some boxes painted with advertisements for your cigars, and you employ several German-Jewish teenagers to sell the boxes of cigars around the city. Workers are happy to buy your cigars—three for two cents and two cents each for the bigger ones. Your profits increase.

One day, as you stand looking over your workshop, you hear a sound you had not noticed before. Perhaps the coughing was always there; in fact, as you remember your days as a worker in the same factory, you recall how others became ill from breathing the tobacco dust. Now, you hear that same coughing, only louder. A woman cigar roller dashes outside from her seat, and you can see that she is coughing, coughing up blood from her lungs and throat.

The sight and sound make you ill, and you turn away. How has it been possible, you wonder, that my own workers, people I know and care about, can be so sick—and I didn't even notice?

Turn to page 124.

69

What kind of store should you open? As you walk down the street, you notice that there are many children in your neighborhood. Wouldn't it be fun to run a toy store where these children and their parents could come and shop? And that's what you do.

The toy store is a success. During the cold Cleveland winters, you sell sleds and ice skates. Parents ask you where to find furniture for their children's rooms. You tell them that you will soon be carrying that kind of merchandise as well. The toy store becomes the furniture and toy store, and people come from great distances to shop there because you and the clerks are always friendly, trying to help them find just the right things.

A policeman comes into the store one day. "Say," he says, "there's a bit of a traffic jam out front. All these folks have come in carriages. They can't leave their horses out in the street." "Of course," you reply at once, "we'll add something new: a stable, where their horses can be fed and groomed."

And so it goes, success after success. There's only one dream left to accomplish. You loved the clean air of "The Heights." Someday, perhaps many years from now, the furniture and toy store and the stable will move up the hill, back into that beautiful part of Cleveland. Then, you will really be content.

END

70

Hebrew Union College is not a very impressive school. Many of the students are much younger than you; some are teenagers; only a few have already graduated from college. Every afternoon, the students gather in a few rooms in the basement of a west Cincinnati temple. When you are finished studying, the entire library is locked in a trunk so the mice don't eat the books!

You and three others become the first rabbis to graduate from Hebrew Union College. You accept the invitation of a congregation in Kansas City to be its rabbi, and you find your chosen career very satisfying. Later, a larger congregation in Philadelphia asks you to move there. Despite the many friends you have made in Kansas City, this is an offer you cannot turn down. It will give you a chance to have more influence than you had in the West.

As the years pass, you remember how much you loved being at college, and you determine to help other Jewish immigrants have that same joy. With others, you found the Jewish Farm School in Doylestown, Pennsylvania, a school where young people can learn the most modern techniques of agriculture. Your efforts help many newcomers enjoy fruitful lives in America.

END

71

When you arrive in Salt Lake City, you find two large groups of people, Indians and Mormons. Both have been treated as outcasts by other Americans, and that mutual experience of discrimination has led them to live together in peace. The Mormons greet you warmly. They think of you as a descendant of the biblical Israelites; in their eyes, this makes you special.

Outside Salt Lake City, you open a trading post, where members of the Ute Tribe can come to buy what they need at a fair and honest price. Not all Indian agents treat their customers with dignity, but you determine that you, a member of a group that has not received respect from others, will never behave toward others as they have behaved toward Jews.

Mormons, Indians, and Jews—what a strange combination! But it works. You spend less and less time at your trading post and more and more time helping different groups in the city get along together. That's fine with you. You feel that your life will have meaning and importance if you can be one of those people who brings peace to the community. It is in the pursuit of *shalom,* "peace," that you spend the rest of your life.

END

72

To your great surprise, you find a small Jewish community in Nacogdoches. They are glad to have you settle with them, and they ask you what kind of work you would enjoy. You tell them about the squabbles among factions of the Jewish community in New Orleans and explain that you would like to be away from people for a while.

"We have just the job for you! Some of us have purchased large tracts of land outside Nacogdoches. We need someone to survey what we own. Can you do that for us?"

You know as much about surveying as you know about flying to the moon, but you can't think of a better opportunity. "Of course I can do that. It sounds like just the right job for me."

You travel through eastern Texas, learning the surveyor's trade from others as you go. From time to time, you come upon a piece of land that no one seems to own. When this happens, you go to the county courthouse as quickly as you can and claim the land for yourself. Over ten years, you amass a considerable holding of land.

But your life is empty. You have avoided people for too long. Now, you must find a larger community in which to settle. You move to Houston, a rapidly growing city. You spend the rest of your life managing your east Texas land holdings and helping to establish a strong and exciting Jewish community.

END

73

It seems that you have already gained a reputation as a fair and honest person. What even Sutro does not realize is that you are also stubborn and will not tolerate crooks. With the help of a judge, who is as unwilling as you to accept illegal behavior, you begin to clean up the city.

Soon your jail is filled with unpleasant characters. Some of them will stay with you only a short time and then be escorted out of town. "Better not show your face around here again," you tell them. "Next time, we won't be so nice." Others face the "hanging judge" and discover they are at the end of their rope. Rather quickly, your reputation spreads; fewer undesirables show up in Virginia City.

Sutro and the leading citizens of the town honor you. They are pleased with the job you have done, and they offer you a lifetime position, which you accept. As sheriff, you enjoy standing for law and order. Being on the side of good and right gives you the feeling that you are making a real difference. You have accomplished something worthwhile; you have lived a satisfying life.

END

74

They were right! You can hardly believe it, but, from the moment you open your store's front door, customers come in and buy your goods. If you have any problem, it is finding enough stock to satisfy the demands of those who want to buy. You are a huge success.

Sometimes farmers and craftsmen come into your store to buy tools. But they cannot always pay you at that moment. "I'll pay you when I harvest my crops." "You'll get your money back when I'm paid for my labor on the house I'm building." You've known many of these men for a long time; they are honest and hardworking; you trust them. So, you give them the tools and other things they need on credit. They sign the ledger, indicating they owe you the money. You really aren't worried. You know that they will pay. Meanwhile, your credit will help them work and earn money, support their families, and build the community.

Turn to page 125.

75

You open a dress shop on the main square of Marion, across from the courthouse. People are glad to have your store there because it is the only one. They are happy to have somewhere to buy clothing. You marry and raise a family.

As your children reach their teenage years, however, you do not want them to sell clothing. You want them to have the chance you never had, the opportunity to go to college. But where? The nearest university is in South Bend, a Catholic school called Notre Dame. It opened only recently, and its representatives have been traveling around the area, trying to recruit new students.

One day, you and the family pile into your new carriage. The horse trots gracefully up the dirt road until you approach South Bend. There, the road changes: two long, parallel rows of wood planks are laid neatly where the carriage wheels should roll. You ride smoothly into South Bend.

At the university, you explain to the admissions officer that your children are Jewish. You do not want them to feel any pressure because the school is Catholic. They assure you that your children will be welcome and that they will be able to live with a Jewish family. That makes you happy.

All your children go to Notre Dame. When your eldest son graduates, he goes to work for the Studebaker Company. Peter and Clem Studebaker had begun with a wagon-making factory. Now, they have heard about a horseless carriage, and they want your son to help them develop one of the first American automobiles. You are very pleased. You have done something very important: You have given your children the opportunity for a better life.

END

76

How strange it feels to be back in Germany! Of course, it is wonderful to see familiar places, to hear the German language, and, especially, to see your family. You study at the university in Berlin and make periodic trips to Neustadt. But you know that this is no longer your country; you are really an American now. You impatiently wait for the two years of training to pass so that you can return to Cincinnati, to the city you now call home.

Crossing the Atlantic going west for the second time is a completely different journey. The first time, you were a teenager and had no money; you slept on the floor and ate whatever you could find. Now, you are a respected professional. The captain of the ship invites you to eat at his table. Other passengers talk with you and ask your advice.

When you return to Cincinnati, you enter medical practice and are almost at once a great success. You attain high status and considerable prestige, not to mention financial wealth. Your life seems complete until . . . until one afternoon, there is a knock on your office door. It is Rabbi Wise. "I hope you are not ill, Rabbi," you quickly say. "Oh, no! Not at all. I am here on business. Do you remember when you wanted to become a rabbi and I told you there was no school in America? Now, it is time to create such a school. I need your help. You must become one of its leaders."

How ironic! You had to return to Germany to study medicine because you couldn't become a rabbi. Now, your medicine will help other young people study for the rabbinate. You immediately accept Rabbi Wise's challenge. The Hebrew Union College will grow from your efforts and the efforts of others like you. Your life will now be complete.

END

Y ou become the boss of a huge freight operation. Hundreds of mules pull dozens of wagons from Missouri across the Great Plains, then south along the Santa Fe Trail into New Mexico. The trip is dangerous; it takes months to cross this great expanse, often through the territory of hostile Indians and murderous bandits. The Army protects the wagon trains as much as it can, but sometimes that is not enough, and all is lost.

On the *High Holy Days* and *Pesach*, you, the Spiegelbergs, your families, and the few other Jews in the territory gather in the biggest of their homes and conduct services. No one dreams of *kosher* food, and the *seder* is hardly like those you experienced in Neustadt when you were young. But you do the best you can. Everyone is happy to be able to have some kind of Jewish celebration.

As you bring your life to a close, you think about what you want inscribed on your tombstone. It's an easy choice for you. You want them to write: "Helped Bring Civilization to the West."

E N D

78

Just as you arrive in Denver, news breaks that silver has been discovered near the town of Leadville. Adventurers, honest and crooked, pour into the region. Everyone has dreams of huge fortunes, of money lying almost on the surface of the ground. In fact, of course, extracting the silver is extremely hard work, and most people leave Leadville no better off than when they arrived.

Otto Mears, a recent Russian immigrant, tells you that he has an idea. He wants to build a railroad up the mountain, a narrow gauge track that will make it possible for people to get to Leadville easily and for riches to return to Denver more quickly. You agree to join him in his efforts. With the help of Ute Indian workers, the railroad moves forward. Unfortunately, Mears runs out of money, and the effort goes bankrupt.

You return to Denver, join the lodge of *B'nai B'rith* and Temple Emanuel, and open a grocery and liquor store. After all the adventures you have had, it feels good to live a normal life, to marry and raise children, and to be a respected member of the community. You feel fortunate: You had adventure; now you have stability. It has been the best of both possible worlds.

END

79

By the time you arrive in Prescott, the *Goldwater* brothers, Morris, Henry, and Baron, have started a general merchandise store. They ask you to direct a special project.

"There are people all over the Arizona Territory who want to start businesses: ranching, mining, all sorts of businesses. But they don't have the money to pay for the basic equipment and supplies they need to start. We can help. Your job will be to talk to these folks. Make judgments. Decide which ones will likely succeed and which ones will probably fail. When you find a good risk, we shall advance whatever they need, and they will promise us five percent of the profits they make."

You are flattered that the *Goldwater* brothers are willing to risk their money on your judgment. And, it seems, their judgment was good. You make good decisions, and most of the investments pay off. They become very wealthy, and so do you.

As you look back on your life, however, it's not the money you remember. You think about the families you were able to help. That is what makes you feel you made a real contribution to your fellow human beings.

E N D

80

As General Grant's army occupies the region around Holly Springs, his officers have heard stories that trading continues between the Union and the Confederacy. That is strictly forbidden. The rumors about dishonest Jewish businessmen find their way into the Northern army headquarters, and soon something terrible happens.

By General Grant's order, General Order No. 11 expels all Jews from the area occupied by the Army of the Tennessee. It does not matter whether the individual Jews were violating trading laws or not; they are expelled as a total group. Within twenty-four hours, you, your family, and your Jewish friends are required to be out of town, on your way back north of the Ohio River. It simply isn't fair.

When you and your friends reach the town of Evansville, Indiana, you meet with some of the Jewish leaders. Caesar Kaskel from Paducah, Kentucky—just across the Ohio River—responds loudly when he hears this story. "This is an outrage! This is exactly what we left behind in Europe. America must be different. We shall not put up with this kind of treatment."

Turn to page 126.

81

While you are beginning to establish yourself as a new resident of Vicksburg, a heated controversy breaks out in the Jewish community there. You know, of course, that there have been arguments for years on the slavery issue. But now this issue intrudes upon the Jewish community. A rabbi from New York, Morris J. Raphall, has written that the Bible endorses slavery and that God has never revealed a change in that attitude. Immediately, Michael Heilprin, a Polish-born journalist now writing in America, challenges Raphall. Other rabbis, like David Einhorn of Baltimore, preach vehemently against slavery. The war of words becomes almost vicious.

In every gathering of Jews in Vicksburg, Jews debate the issue. Some think that slavery is the only way the South can survive; others believe that slavery is wrong. Even they, however, don't like the idea of Northerners telling them what to do. "If we want to change our system," they say, "that should be our business. And we have to do it slowly, gradually." The discussions are heated; angry words are often exchanged, and you wonder where you yourself stand on this issue.

If you decide that the South should control its own destiny,
turn to page 83.

If you side with the antislavery group,
turn to page 90.

If you decide not to become involved in this argument,
turn to page 95.

82

The Jewish community of Virginia, Minnesota, grows. A synagogue building is erected; from time to time, you are even able to find a rabbi who will come to this small city and conduct services for you.

You never marry. There just aren't many Jews your age available, and even trips into Milwaukee and Chicago don't work. You think about marrying someone much younger but decide against that idea.

"After all," you write to your family in Neustadt, "I may not have had any children of my own, but all your children are really my family. They have come here from Germany, grown up to be Americans, and are now taking an active part in building this wonderful country. And they have remained Jews. Here, far from the cities, we have a fine little Jewish community. We are very proud of what we have accomplished, and I feel immensely satisfied with my life. What more could I have asked, after all, than to be surrounded by young people who love me and whose lives I have changed for the better! It has been a wonderful life."

E N D

83

A Southern patriot can do only one thing: enlist in the army of the Confederate States of America—and that is exactly what you do. You are assigned to Company F of Wither's Artillery, a special unit of Mississippi soldiers. You train hard; cannonballs from your unit's guns fall closer to their targets than those of other units; your *esprit de corps* is very high.

Word comes to your headquarters that General Sherman's army is advancing on Atlanta, Georgia. Wither's Artillery is one of the units dispatched to stop his forward march. You establish your line of defense northwest of the city at a place called Kenesaw Mountain. It is there that you and the others will take your stand in defense of your homeland and the Southern way of life.

Sherman's advance, however, cannot be halted. As accurate as your artillery fire is, his much larger army moves forward. Soon, his infantry soldiers leap over the earthwork barriers that you had dug to protect your position. They fire their muskets toward you and pierce others with their bayonets. The last thing you feel is a stabbing pain as the saber of a Union officer enters your chest. You have fought a good fight; now it is over.

END

84

When you arrive in San Diego, you take a room in a boarding house. At night, you stroll around the waterfront, looking at the boats and talking to the interesting men who sail off on them for months at a time. Every sight is new and exciting to you, and you almost forget that you need to find a job if you are to stay in this community.

Naturally, you go to the synagogue. Where else would a Jew find other Jews and the advice they can give about settling down? The *vestry* of the *shul* is meeting as you enter. "We have a terrible problem. Some of the men who arrive in San Diego on the fishing boats are Jewish. They have little money, certainly not enough to bring their families to join them. It's our obligation to shelter them and get them on their feet. That's a basic *mitzvah*. But how shall we proceed?"

You raise your hand and make a suggestion. "Perhaps you could start a Hebrew Benevolent Society as they have done in other cities. Every member contributes a little each week. Pretty soon, you would have enough money to help these needy people."

Everyone applauds. What a wonderful idea! All of a sudden, you find yourself elected secretary of the H.B.S. of San Diego. It's a surprise, but a pleasant one—one you can certainly live with for the rest of your life.

END

85

You return to San Francisco. As you step off the stage-coach, there is a commotion near the depot. A tall man with a huge mustache is making a speech. He looks like some kind of military officer—formal blue uniform with lots of gold trim, sword hung on his left hip, tall hat decked out with feathers.

"Who is this person?" you ask the woman standing next to you. "Oh, that's the crazy Jew, Joshua Norton. He calls himself Emperor Norton I. Years ago, I understand, he had some money. But he lost it investing in rice. He became very unbalanced. Now, he even issues his own money. People don't take him very seriously, but kind merchants and restaurant owners accept his money for food and lodging. He's a local character."

He certainly is! But you must move on. You find a job and start your family, settling down to a more predictable and stable life. One day, some of your friends propose that you start a new lodge of the Jewish fraternal order *B'nai B'rith.* It sounds like a good idea, and you agree. It would be nice to have a Jewish club where you could talk over important matters together.

The lodge opens. You suggest a name: *Ophir,* the biblical land of gold. You may not have found a golden fortune in Eureka, but you will always be able to enter your lodge and shout: "Eureka! Land of Gold, I am here!"

END

86

You journey east from San Francisco to Sacramento. There, you find a job in the dry goods store of Lubin and Weinstock. More interesting than the store, however, are the political discussions these two committed Jews and liberals have. They are always talking about how they can help the "common man," the average person. For one thing, they have put tags on every item in the store with the fixed price—no bargaining, no raising prices for some customers and lowering them for others, the way some businessmen do. They run an honest and fair store.

Lubin, however, is not content to stay in Sacramento. He wants to change the way farmers all over the world grow their crops; he thinks there is a more scientific way to run a farm. One day, when there are no customers in the store, he reads you the story of *Ruth* from the Bible—how Jews always were concerned that everyone had enough to eat and how they would leave part of their harvest for the poor. "I've got to fulfill this old Jewish idea that everyone would have enough food."

Lubin leaves for Italy. He has managed to convince King Victor Emmanuel to help him establish an International Institute for Agriculture. His letters arrive from time to time, telling you of his work. You remain with Harris Weinstock and run the store. You feel satisfied that you have freed David Lubin to become, as he himself said, "a successor to the ancient Jewish prophets." In your small way, you have helped make his dreams come true; perhaps in some fashion you have been a helper to a modern-day prophet.

END

87

To brew beer, you must have lots of grain. You can generally rely on a steady stream of loaded wagons from the Minnesota and Dakota prairies. But suppose there is a bad harvest, or an Indian attack, or the farmers decide to ship their harvest elsewhere. No, you cannot build a business unless you have an assured supply.

You do two things. First, you go to the bank and secure a loan to build a huge grain elevator. The three tall, circular tubes rise into the cold northern sky, ready to receive and store thousands of bushels of the precious grain. Then, you make a trip to the farms. At each one, you offer the same proposition: "If you will guarantee to bring your harvest to me, I will guarantee to purchase it." It's a good deal for you and for the farmers, and most of them readily agree.

When you return to St. Paul, your future seems settled. You have assured the success of your brewery, and now you can turn to other matters. Life has been good to you; now you want to return the favors. And, during the next decades, you spend most of your time searching out ways to do *tzedakah,* to help those in the city who have not been as fortunate as you. (And you do it privately, without telling anyone.) One *Shabbat* morning, in the synagogue, you think to yourself: God has given me many blessings; at least I have been thankful enough to pass some of them on to other people. I know in my heart that I have tried to do the right thing.

END

88

Most of the new immigrants who arrive in Milwaukee are from Eastern Europe. They speak only *Yiddish,* making it difficult to communicate with other people in the city. In addition, their customs are different from those of the German Jews so that they appear very strange, both to Jews and non-Jews alike.

You and the other leaders of the Jewish community decide to help these new residents learn how to become Americans. You want them to settle into the life of the city easily and quickly. "What we should do," someone says at a meeting, "is create a place where they can learn English and learn to behave properly. Doesn't the Torah teach us that *we should be kind to strangers* because our people were once strangers in the land of Egypt? Let's call the place a 'settlement house' because we want them to settle into America."

And so the Abraham Lincoln Settlement House is founded. Immigrant Jews can come there, learn English, get help with money, food, clothing, and coal for their stoves, and even receive assistance in finding a job. You all contribute money for the effort, but it's never enough. One of the leaders of the Abraham Lincoln Settlement House, Mrs. Simon Kander, gets a brilliant idea: "Let's make up a cookbook and sell it. The money we take in will really help. You immediately assist her, collecting recipes and arranging the pages. The settlement cookbook becomes a best seller. You are very proud that you helped make it possible for so many immigrant Jews to find new homes and make their futures in America.

END

89

A small Jewish community like Madison can only afford one religious professional. You must become a *kol bo,* someone who does everything. At times, you become the *chazan,* who leads services; at other times, you are the *mohel* or the *shochet;* parents ask you to serve as the *melamed,* who prepares their sons for *bar mitzvah*—you really do perform every task.

And you love it. These are wonderful people. Sometimes, of course, they have differences and get into arguments. Everyone has his or her own opinion about each issue. But deep down they are tied together by a bond that cannot be broken—a bond of common heritage that goes all the way back to the time the Israelites stood before Sinai and received the Torah.

These are your people. You left Milwaukee to live in a community where people know one another. You have been lucky to find such a place. Madison's Jews have an intimate, intense relationship with one another, and you feel extremely fortunate to be included.

END

As a Jew, as someone who has experienced anti-Semitism in Europe, as someone whose father was prevented from taking certain jobs, from owning land, from being a full part of society, you simply cannot agree that other people, whatever their color, should be treated as slaves. The message of the *Pesach seder* keeps coming back to you: "We were slaves in Egypt, and that was not a pleasant experience. It was so awful that God heard our cries and saved us. If it was not good for us, slavery cannot be acceptable for anyone."

You join those who speak against slavery. Soon, however, you discover that you are in a small minority, even among the Jews of Vicksburg. Many of them earn a great deal of money from businesses that trade with slave plantations, and they are unwilling to challenge a system that has been good for them and their families. "Where," they ask, "do you think the money that we used to ransom you came from?"

You and the others who oppose slavery become unpopular. Word of your stand becomes known among the non-Jews as well, and you are taunted and harassed as you walk down the street. Soon it becomes apparent that you cannot stay in Vicksburg; you must leave. The Great Lakes region appeals to you, and you travel to the city of Cleveland on the southern shore of Lake Erie.

Turn to page 15.

91

You make a lot of money. With some of the profits from the business, you buy apartment buildings. However, the depression of 1873 takes its toll, and people do not have money to pay their rents. Although you lose some of your money, you do survive. At age 55, you have enough money to retire.

Eastern European Jewish immigrants arriving in Chicago are attacked with anti-Semitic slander. While these new people are very different from us, you think, they are still Jewish, still our people. We have an obligation to defend them—and ourselves.

You dedicate yourself to the well-being of these new immigrants, helping them become Americans and protecting them from the rumors and charges that some people make against them and against all Jews. This work gives you a tremendous sense of satisfaction; you have made a good choice.

END

92

When you arrive on the banks of the Mississippi River, you are hungry and thirsty. It has been a long and tiring trip from Chicago. You head for the nearest saloon, Bush's Tavern, and order food and drink. The owner comes over to your table. "You're new in town, aren't you? *Bist du a landsman?*" You cannot believe your ears. You have been in St. Louis less than one hour and already you are sitting with the Jewish owner of a tavern who wants to know if you are also Jewish. Destiny must have led you here.

You introduce yourself to Isidore Bush and tell him that you desperately need a place to stay and a job. He offers you hospitality. ("Hachnasat orechim, 'welcoming guests,' is a *mitzvah,*" he reminds you.) He makes arrangements for you to work in the vineyards that he owns outside town.

While the job is not very exciting, the city is. When you have time off, you stroll along the waterfront. When the steamboats dock, there is always commotion, noise, and excitement; interesting characters come ashore. One of the most unusual is a stern-wheeler pilot, *Samuel Clemens.* *Clemens* is also a writer. He uses the pen name of Mark Twain, and now he shows you something he has written about Jews. You read the words carefully. The Jew "is as prominent on the planet as any other people. . . . His contributions to the world's list of great names . . . are also way out of proportion to the weakness of his numbers."

You feel proud. An author you respect has praised you and your people. You lean back against Bush's bar and smile. It feels good to be a Jew.

END

93

On a windy, blustery March day, you go to the bank where you have all your savings. You sit with the president of the bank and explain your plan to invest in a new steel mill. "I use lots of steel in my business. If I had a mill nearby, instead of bringing it all the way from Pittsburgh, I could make a much larger profit. If the bank will lend me enough money to get started, we will both be very rich."

The banker agrees. You take your money as well as the bank's and build a small steel mill that can produce the kind of reinforcing rods that you require. The mill opens in November, and you eagerly await the first ship with iron ore from the new mines in Minnesota. Unfortunately for you, this is going to be one of the coldest winters in history. Lake Michigan actually freezes over, and the ships cannot sail from Duluth to East Chicago.

"We loaned you a lot of money," your banker says. "You promised to pay us back every month. It is already April, and you have not yet made one payment." You explain your problems to the bank president, but he is not interested in listening. The bank seizes your mill, and you lose all the money that you had personally invested in it. You are broke!

You may be financially ruined, but you have not given up on your vision. "If I cannot get the iron ore here, I shall go where it is. Somehow, I will make my future in this business."

Turn to page 18.

94

You cannot believe that children—young boys and girls under thirteen years of age—go into the mine shafts each day. They do not actually dig, but they help carry messages and food to the miners. Some days they work twelve hours. They come out of the tunnels covered with coal dust. They are paid only pennies. When the shafts cave in or when there is an explosion, children are killed along with the miners.

You are appalled. "In this modern age, these young children should not be working like this. They ought to be in school, learning to read and write and do their sums, not risking their lives in the mines. It's only because the mining companies refuse to pay their parents a decent wage that they are forced to work and add whatever they can to the family's income."

You cannot accept this situation. Some miners consider forming a union, but even talking about it is dangerous. People have been killed by company thugs just for thinking like that. But you become convinced that unions and government laws that regulate child labor are absolutely necessary. Very quietly, you become a supporter of this movement. Over the years, you become even more committed to the cause. Eventually, you devote almost all your time to changing the conditions under which these workers and their families toil. When you came to America, other people helped you better your life; now, it is your turn to return the favor. These men, women, and children will, you predict, be safer and more secure because of your efforts, and that makes you feel very good.

END

95

The Jews of Vicksburg were kind to you; they saved you from the bandits who had kidnapped you, paying a considerable ransom. If you take an antislavery position, you will embarrass them—something you do not want to do. On the other hand, you cannot bring yourself to endorse a system that keeps human beings in chains. Your conscience will not allow you to support slavery, especially when you remember that Jews have often been treated like slaves during the centuries.

The only honorable path for you is to leave quietly and find a place where the controversy is less heated. That's, however, easier to say than to do. The entire country is consumed by this debate. In the North, abolitionists speak in every city and town, denouncing the South and encouraging a war to free the slaves. Southerners speak just as strongly in defense of their system and assure the North that they will fight for their way of life, even if it means military conflict.

The people who live west of the Mississippi are so busy developing their new towns and businesses that they have less time for arguments about slavery. Of course, they do care, one way or another, sometimes intensely, but their main interest is making a new life for themselves on the frontier. You begin to believe that the West is the region where you should be making a new start for yourself.

Turn to page 120.

96

Adolph Ochs has just purchased a newspaper in New York City. The *New York Times* is not doing very well at this time, but he has the ambition to make it the best newspaper in the world. To do that, he wants to surround himself with young, energetic, intelligent reporters and editors. You are extremely flattered that he has considered you.

You accept his offer although you do not remember New York with great fondness. "I guess I can be happy anywhere if I am doing something important, something I believe in." (In later years, you will wonder if this was really a smart thing to say, but, of course, then it is too late.)

The *New York Times* takes a long time to become established. You grow old, working on the paper, watching it slowly succeed—but only slowly. Still, it is good to know that you were there at the beginning. And when it is recognized as the very best, you will be able to say: "I was one of the people who made this possible."

END

97

At the prison camp, some wounded soldiers lie on the ground. Others walk on crutches. Some have filthy bandages on their heads or arms. There are no sanitary conditions; dirt is everywhere. You are sure that an epidemic of disease will break out.

You ask for an appointment with the camp commander. "Sir, I know that you do not have enough soldiers to help our wounded. But I can. Did you know that my friend, *David de Leon,* is the surgeon-general of the Confederate army? [You don't even know *de Leon,* but you speak with confidence, hoping that the commander will not challenge your bluff.] If you would give me permission, I would even treat the sick and wounded among your soldiers."

With nothing to lose, the commander appoints you medical director. You spend the rest of the war trying to make life more comfortable for the wounded and ill. You cannot do much, but whatever you do is better than what would have been done.

After the war, you think about your experiences. You loved the South, but they started a war that led to extraordinary misery and death. You are proud to live in America, but there are many things wrong with this country. It's all so confusing. You cannot think of anywhere in this country that you would be comfortable and happy.

Finally, however, you decide to stay in the South. You spend the rest of your life trying to understand a war that makes no sense to you.

END

98

You leave Talbottom on horseback. After you cross the Mississippi River on a flat-bottomed barge, you join others who are journeying west on the Santa Fe Trail that leads into the Arizona Territory. You see few white people during this trip, but there are enough signs of Indian life to keep you alert. Later you learn that most of these Native Americans are peaceful and friendly; only the Apaches and a few other tribes are hostile.

In the San Francisco mountains of southeastern Arizona, a small mining industry already exists. Copper and other metals have been discovered, and rumors tell of huge fortunes to be made. You have no one other than yourself to care for. Why not give adventure a try? You leave the Santa Fe Trail and head for the mining camps.

The work is backbreaking, and the rewards are far less than you had imagined. One evening in a saloon, you meet a new arrival, Henry Lesinsky. This Jew from western Poland is more intense than any man you have ever met. He has a goal, and nothing will prevent him from reaching it. He and the Freudenthal brothers have staked a claim they call the Longfellow Mine. They are sure there is a huge amount of copper there.

You come to believe in Lesinsky and his dream. You work at the Longfellow. It takes a long time, but, eventually, Lesinsky's hopes pay off—and so does your hard labor. You are able to retire to Las Cruces, New Mexico, with enough money to last the rest of your life and with the knowledge that you and the others had helped "open up the West."

END

99

You work very hard in the cigar factory—ten hours a day, twelve hours a day. On weekends, you volunteer to come in and sweep the floor. It seems that there is nothing in your life but work and eating and sleeping. Some of your coworkers wonder why you are slaving so hard. "Why are you driving yourself? Have a little fun once in a while."

You don't tell them, but you've got a secret plan. Every penny, every dollar you do not spend goes into a special bank account. Because you work so hard, the balance grows rapidly, and soon you have enough. Enough for what?

You write a letter back to Neustadt. "Mother and Father, this land has been good to me. I have been able to find good work, a fine place to live, nice friends, and an active Jewish community. It's not like Neustadt, but now it's my home. I miss you and my brothers and sisters very much. I have now saved up a sum of money. It's not enough to bring all of you here at once, but some of you can come. Then, we can all save to bring the others. In a short time, all of our family will be together again. Please write back and say that you accept this idea. Your loving child."

Your parents write back immediately. Soon two of your brothers arrive in Cleveland. The plan works. They save their money, and, within a year, the rest of your family comes to the New World. It has been seven years since you left Neustadt, but, as you and your family recline at the *Pesach seder,* you think back: Once we lived in slavery; now we are free. *Baruch Atah Adonai,* praised be God who has allowed us to come to this land of liberty.

END

100

Every day, more immigrant Jews from Eastern Europe arrive in Cleveland. Some of them have terrible problems. They or their children become ill. Sometimes, a member of the family dies, and they fall into deep poverty. They cannot speak English or manage in such a strange and new land.

These people need the help of a person like you, a person who now understands American ways and has made a place for himself in this country. You secure a position with the Hebrew Benevolent Society, a group that is dedicated to helping new immigrants succeed here. Every day, you visit the boarding houses and apartments where the immigrants live, teaching them new skills and helping them to secure enough to eat, to find jobs, to remain healthy, and to become Americans.

Over the years, you help many people. You have found a career that has satisfied you greatly. As you look back over a long life of important work, you remember the words of *Pirke Avot:* "If you save even one person, it is as though you had saved the entire world." You think to yourself: I have saved many people; I have lived a good and worthwhile life.

END

101

Now that you are older and more confident, you return to Ohio State University and pursue a graduate degree in classical languages. You continue to study Hebrew, adding Greek and Latin. After a number of years, you receive a doctor of philosophy degree. Now, you are ready to teach in any of the finest universities in the land.

One of your faculty advisors has heard that a particular university is looking for a teacher with your qualifications. He recommends that you apply. In a few weeks, you receive a letter, inviting you to come for an interview. The committee is courteous and attentive as you answer all their questions. You think you did pretty well, and you are confident as you leave the room. As you sit in the hallway, however, you hear the chairman of the committee: "A Jew! We shall have no Jews on this faculty. That's the end of the discussion!"

You leave immediately. What a terrible, sick feeling you have in your stomach. To have worked so hard, so successfully, and now to be rejected just because of your religion. You had never realized that there was so much anti-Semitism in America.

With the help of some friends and many rabbis, you become active with the *Board of Delegates of American Israelites.* In 1878, it becomes the social action arm of the new *Union of American Hebrew Congregations.* You spend the rest of your life with this organization, speaking up for Jews, protecting their rights and privileges here in America and in other countries. No work, you think to yourself, could ever be more important.

END

102

As you arrive in Omaha, you pick up a copy of a newspaper called the "Evening Bee." What a surprise to see that the name of the publisher is Edward Rosewater—he must be a Jew! You seek him out at his offices and discover that he is a fighter against the powerful railroad interests and a crusader against crooks. He is for the rights of common people, for public schools, and for public libraries.

Rosewater's friend, Max Meyer, hires you to help him sell musical instruments, but this business is limited. You would rather work in the general store of Max's brother, Julius, the one the Indians call "Curly-Haired-White Chief with One Tongue."

With the Meyer brothers and Rosewater, you spend much of your time defending Jewish rights on the frontier. You are a founding member of the Omaha lodge of *B'nai B'rith,* and you later become president of the Jewish Cemetery Association. Luck and your own abilities have helped you become a leader in this Jewish community and a respected citizen in Omaha. As you grow old, you look back: "I've come a long way from Neustadt, but look what great adventures I have had. Thank You, God, for keeping me alive, for preserving me, and for permitting me to reach this time of success and happiness in my life."

END

103

The city of Dallas is actually a few dirt streets lined with wood frame houses and stores. As you walk down the main street, however, you see a sign over a general store: Sanger Brothers. You wonder if Jews have reached this far west.

Of course! A city such as Dallas that is rapidly becoming a center for railroad transportation attracts energetic, enterprising people. The whole Sanger family has come over from Bavaria, first to New York, then to McKinney and Corsicana, Texas, and other smaller towns, and finally to Dallas. You find a place to live and accept a job with their company.

The weather is beastly hot during the summer, pleasant during most of the rest of the year, except when a "Blue Norther" sweeps through, dropping the temperature well below freezing. Still, you love Dallas. There's something about the place and its people, something that says: "We're building the future. It may not always go smoothly, but we're going to be bigger and better and greater." You are glad to be part of this progress. It's exciting. It is certainly where you want to spend the rest of your life.

E N D

The miners all have pockets full of money. You want some of it for yourself. With a partner, you open a saloon and opera house, a place where the workers can come after a long week of labor, have something to eat and drink, and see a show. The piano player and the dancing girls are local talent—not bad, but local—but you also bring in well-known, touring actors, musicians, and singers.

One of the highlights is the week *Adah Isaacs Menken* comes to town. This internationally-known actress captures the hearts of all who see her. When she takes her final bow, the audience throws bags of gold dust onto the stage. An entire mining district is named in her honor. Even Mark Twain, then a writer for the local paper, is captivated by her.

After a number of years, the veins of ore under the mountains are exhausted. A few miners still work the hills, but most have moved on to new areas: Colorado, Montana, Alaska. Your fancy opera house is now only a simple restaurant. It will hardly produce enough money to support you and your family.

You conclude that you must move away from this declining city. Reluctantly, you load your family and belongings into a wagon and start down the west side of the Sierras toward San Francisco.

Turn to page 35.

105

People buy clothing from your store. Slowly, you accumulate a good deal of money, but one thing bothers you. You remember that your father and mother in Germany were always suspicious of the non-Jewish bankers in Neustadt. They told you: "Give them your money, and you'll never see it again. Somehow they'll find a way to steal it from you." Of course, this is America, a very different world. Where can you put all your savings?

One summer day, a cart pulls up to your store. It is the cart from the Abraham Kuhn Company in Cincinnati, loaded with your new stock of shirts and trousers. The driver stays overnight with you. Because he is also from Germany, you feel you can talk honestly with him. You tell him the problem you are facing. He laughs. "We all have the same problem, my friend. All of us who travel on the road wondered what to do with our money. Then we got a good idea. We went to Papa Kuhn and asked him to hold the money for us. He agreed and appointed one of his sons as our private banker. When we get to Cincinnati after a long trip, we give him the money. We trust him. He gives us a receipt, and every month our accounts grow. Why don't you do the same thing?"

He's right. At the earliest moment, you travel to Cincinnati and deposit your savings with the Kuhn bank. After a few years, you read that the Kuhns have relocated the bank to New York City, the capital of America's financial world. They have gone into partnership with a famous American-German Jewish family, the Loebs. As you grow older, you are pleased that some of your money helped establish *Kuhn, Loeb, and Company.* It's almost as if you were related to the *Rothschilds.*

END

106

You travel northward, through Illinois, Wisconsin, and Minnesota, until you come to the town of Yankton, South Dakota. It is so cold here that the winter wind slices through your coat as if you had nothing on. Still, when you look around, you see hundreds of Scandinavian men, some with their families. Every one of them will need to buy something; surely, this will be a good place for a successful store.

Your general store sells almost everything. From buttons and clothing to hardware and tools and pots and pans and . . . just about everything. Because it's the only such store for miles and miles around, everyone comes in. You greet customers with a smile and a polite and respectful manner; you always try to learn their names. They like to come to your store, and, as a result, it succeeds very nicely.

Your family also succeeds. During the course of the next ten or so years, you and your spouse have four children. There is only one problem that the two of you cannot solve: There are no other Jewish families in the region. "How is it possible for our children to continue the tradition that we were taught by our parents? How is it possible for our children to remain Jewish?"

As you drift off to sleep one winter evening, you realize that you have created an impossible dilemma: You love the store in Yankton and all the profits it produces, but you also love being Jewish. Is there any escape from this problem? You doze off. Perhaps tomorrow you will figure out how to solve it.

END

107

In 1861, just as your medical practice begins to succeed, war breaks out between the Northern states and those in the South. Soon, people are calling it the Civil War. Doctors are desperately needed, as young soldiers are wounded in battle.

You cannot stand idly by while the blood of your neighbors is spilled. [Leviticus 19:16] Your conscience will not allow you to remain apart from the suffering of these young men. You enlist in the Grand Army of the Republic and are appointed a surgeon with the rank of major. Your uniform is glorious, with gold buttons, fringed epaulets on your shoulders, and a long, shiny sword.

The glory and glamour do not last long. Almost as soon as you join the army, you are sent to the Seventh Infantry Regiment of General Grant's army in Mississippi. The Confederate forces have been advancing northward through the state, and now there will surely be a battle near the town of Corinth. Tens of thousands of soldiers face one another, and it pains you to wonder how many will not be alive next week, how many will be disabled by the cannons and sabers.

Turn to page 127.

108

You establish a trading post in Apache country. The warriors are frightening to you, but you treat them with respect. They return the favor unless they have been cheated by another white man. . . .

One evening, a band of angry braves breaks into your store, grabs you, and ties you up. They carry you off to their camp and keep you prisoner for several weeks. However, they have one problem: no water. It has not rained in this area for months. Suddenly, you see your chance.

"I know an old rain dance," you tell them. "It has worked many times; I think it will work now." Having nothing to lose, they let you dance Mayim, a water dance. To even your great surprise, a thunderstorm drenches their camp. Impressed, they let you go, and you return to your home. But you have been so scared that you cannot stay in this area. You feel you must move to a location that is more civilized than this. So you uproot yourself once again, now directing your steps toward Virginia City, Nevada.

Turn to page 25.

109

Reports from the summit tell of gold and silver. A group of men in Breckenridge, who wish to stake claim to land in the high mountains, hire you to be their surveyor. They promise that you will have an equal share of any land they acquire and of the ores that come from the mines on that property.

Unfortunately, as soon as you have done your work, they tell you straight to your face: "We're not interested in having any Jews as our partners. Here's a fair wage for your work. Now, get lost!"

There are far too many of them for you to argue. You leave, disappointed, and return to Denver. Even in America, it is sometimes hard to be a Jew or to work for people who are not Jewish. You decide that you will never do that again. You will own your own business. You open a small hotel, which succeeds nicely because Denver is growing, and there are lots of travelers into and through the city.

Several years later, a man comes to rent a room. You recognize him as one of the anti-Semitic men who forced you out of the land holdings at Breckenridge. But he doesn't realize who you are. You are tempted not to take him in. But then you remember a verse from the Torah, "You shall not take vengeance or bear a grudge." [Leviticus 19:18] And you say to yourself with a smile: I could act like him, but I feel better doing the opposite. Then you turn to your guest: "Welcome! But that will be cash in advance!"

END

110

Nathan Bibo of Grants, New Mexico, owns a huge sheep ranch, making a profit on the wool and the meat of these animals.

He has a special relationship with the Acoma Pueblo Indians who work his ranch and consider him a trusted advisor. You join Bibo's Indian herdsmen in caring for the sheep. The days are hot and long, but the nights under the cool, star-filled desert sky are spectacular. On such a night, as you lie looking upward from your bedroll, you remember a verse from the Book of Psalms [8:2] "O great God, You have stamped Your glory in the heavens!"

That ancient Psalmist must have seen the same sky under which you now lie in wonder. You feel a personal connection with the biblical author, and a deep sense of peace comes over you. If you can spend the rest of your life looking up at God's handiwork, you will never wish for anything else. And so it is that you live out your life, completely content, working for the Bibo ranch in northcentral New Mexico.

END

111

In Europe you expected anti-Semitism. That's one of the reasons you came to America. You thought that here people would be judged on their own merits, on what they did, and how they lived, not on the basis of their religion. But, apparently, that is not always the case.

You have heard of an Indian territory west of the Mississippi River, the Oklahoma Territory. Surely, the people living there do not have a tradition of anti-Semitism. If you were to go to live among them, at least you might be spared anti-Jewish abuse. That is where you decide to go.

You settle on a farm in southeastern Oklahoma. True to your expectations, the Indians don't even know what a Jew is, and, as long as you are honest and fair with them, they treat you well. Years pass, and you feel very comfortable living there although you are only a simple dirt farmer.

One day, late in your life, you are plowing in the northern section of your farm. Your mule seems to have trouble walking, and the plow becomes sticky and slips out of the furrows. You wonder what has happened. Then, you look more carefully at the ground. A black, gooey substance is oozing out of the ground. It's oil! You and your family will never want for anything again.

As you sit on the front porch of your home that evening, you think: How strange life is! I fled anti-Semitism in Holly Springs. I found a shelter here in Oklahoma. Now, I have found oil. *Gam zu letovah,* "This, too, has been for the best." Everything has turned out alright.

END

112

After *Havdalah* services at the close of *Shabbat,* you turn to your friends. "I want you to know how deeply I appreciate what you have done for me. I probably would have been killed by those bandits if you had not helped me. I will never forget you. But my future is not in Vicksburg. Because you have a way of life here that I can never share comfortably, I must leave. Tomorrow morning, I shall be on my way, but you will always be in my heart."

On a stern-wheel steamer, loaded with the bales of cotton you used to buy for Seinsheimer, you travel north, up the Mississippi River. Past St. Louis, you continue northward, finally leaving the boat at Davenport, Iowa. A ferry takes you across the river to the Illinois side. From there, you find a wagon that is headed east, and you journey for several days until you come to the city of Chicago.

Chicago is rapidly becoming a major commercial city. Business transactions occur on the street, in stores, in offices, and in homes. Everywhere, people have the attitude that tomorrow will be better, that they can make lots of money, that the future is very bright. This is surely a place where you can make a good life for yourself.

Turn to page 37.

113

"It's a strange idea," your friends tell you, "but why not? You have a fine reputation as an honest person, as someone who will always help a neighbor. Everyone knows you are intelligent, and you have enough money of your own so no one will suspect you of stealing public money. Why not? Yes! You should run for mayor."

You cannot believe that this is possible. In Europe, it would have been unthinkable for a Jew to run, much less be elected, for a position of importance, especially a position in which he would govern non-Jews. But America is not Europe; America is a different country, a different world altogether. In America, Jews and non-Jews live together, work together, even go to one another's homes. Perhaps it is not so strange, after all, that a Jew should consider being mayor of an American city.

You run in the election, and, surprisingly, you are elected. You serve eight years in the position and then retire. It's time for someone else. When you leave city hall, a large testimonial dinner is held in your honor. The most prominent people of St. Paul attend; one after the other, they rise to speak your praises. You look back on your life. You have accomplished a great deal; you have been honored; you are respected. The promise of the New World has, indeed, come true in your days.

END

114

The money you have earned in the funeral home makes it possible for you to buy some apartment buildings. With the rents from them, you are on your way to becoming wealthy. But then you ask yourself: Is this money really mine? Did I create the wood we use for coffins, the stones with which we build the apartments, the air we breathe, the food we eat? We helped, but the raw materials came from somewhere else.

On *Shabbat* morning, as you *daven shacharit,* your mind drifts to a phrase from the Book of Psalms [24:1]. Suddenly, you remember the words: "The earth is God's and all its fullness, the world and all who dwell in it. For God has established it. . . ." "That's right," you exclaim out loud. While the other amazed worshipers stare at you, you jump up and run to the president of the *shul.* "Look, you know I am well-to-do. But what I have earned is really God's money; I used what God created to make money for myself, and now I feel I must give something back. It's time for us to stop meeting for services in the living room of this house. If you will join me, I shall give a very large donation to help build a proper synagogue. The only condition is that the ark be dedicated to the memory of my parents, *alechem hashalom."*

Everyone agrees with great enthusiasm. After *Shabbat*, a planning committee is established with you as chair. Funds are raised, and plans are drawn. Soon, workers begin to raise the walls of the first synagogue building in Milwaukee. You look at the work with contentment; you have done well, but you have also paid a debt to God—and to your parents— through your act of *tzedakah.* Now, you can look back on your entire life with satisfaction. It has all been worthwhile.

END

115

Because no law school has yet been opened at the university, you read law at the office of an older attorney. The course of study is informal; whatever subject he tells you to learn is the next topic. You follow him to court, watch him prepare his own cases, and sit with him when he talks with his clients. After three years, he tells you that you have learned enough to open your own law office.

Over the years, you gain a reputation as a fair, honest, and capable lawyer. One evening after dinner, you and your family are talking in the sitting room of your home. Suddenly, there is a knock on the door. Three leaders of the Wisconsin state government stand outside. You immediately invite them in and offer them refreshments. "We have not come on a social call. You may have heard that Judge Olavson has retired. We need a replacement, and we believe that you are the right person. Will you allow us to have the Wisconsin State Senate appoint you as district judge?"

You are surprised but thrilled, and, of course, you accept. When you lived in Neustadt, the *dayan* of the Jewish community was always its most respected citizen. To be sure, a district judge is not quite the same as the *dayan* of a Jewish *bet din,* but it's close. You never dreamed that you would be able to continue in the same role as all the great talmudic judges of the past. You have moved a long way in your life, but some things have stayed the same, and you are grateful.

E N D

116

Bakersfield is exactly the quiet, peaceful town you had hoped for. Quiet and peaceful, that is, until the ranchers and the farmers begin to fight each other over control of the land and water. Ranchers want open spaces so their sheep can graze anywhere; farmers want fences to protect their crops. Farmers want lots of water to make their plants grow; ranchers control the mountains where the rivers have their sources. The battle goes on and on. Both sides have good arguments, and sometimes they back their positions with rifles and six-guns.

One night, as you are trying to sleep, fighting breaks out outside your home. You throw on a pair of trousers under your nightshirt and dash outside. "Enough! Stop! There's got to be a better way."

You practically push the combatants into your living room, give them coffee and cake, and get them to start talking. By dawn, a compromise has been reached: Some land will be fenced—but not all; some water will be let into the streams—but not too much. Everyone seems pleased that the fighting and killing will cease.

The next day, the townspeople come into the store you now own. "You made peace in our community. We are thankful. Please accept our thanks by becoming Justice of the Peace. We need someone like you to settle disputes."

You accept and spend the rest of your life trying to live up to the honor your neighbors have bestowed upon you.

END

117

You travel up the Pacific coast to Seattle, where you find a job with Lewis Gerstle's Alaska Commercial Company. He has been able to look into the future and predict that there will be considerable trade between Alaska and the United States. Someday, he thinks, America will even own Alaska. I don't know when, but I want to be established in the trading business so that, when it happens, I can take advantage of the new opportunities. You're not sure whether Mr. Gerstle is right or wrong, but he treats you fairly, and the pay is good. You, too, come to have a vision of the future.

One day, you enter his office and make a suggestion. "Mr. Gerstle, I think we ought to go into the fishing business. The Indians along the rivers here catch salmon and smoke them. If we could have some ships go out into the ocean and catch salmon, we could smoke them the same way. Jews certainly love smoked salmon; I think we could convince other Americans to eat it, too."

Gerstle tilts his head to one side, then to the other. *"Lox? Lox?* Why not? We could become the *lox* kings of the world. I think that's a great idea. Go ahead. God bless you in this new endeavor."

Your salmon fishing venture is a tremendous success. *Lox* from your smokehouses is sent all over the country, and, as you look back over a long life, you have the satisfaction of knowing that you have changed the way Americans eat. You pat yourself on the stomach and say: "That was certainly a good life."

END

118

Sherith Israel is more friendly and less formal than Emanu-El. You hold your services in the living room of someone's home, as you cannot possibly afford to build a separate building. That will come later; for now, it is simply enough to pray with your new friends, although you are German and they are Polish.

One afternoon, during the holiday of *Sukot,* you and the others are sitting in the *sukah.* You look across at one of the men and notice he is wearing some very unusual pants. They are made of heavy blue material, sewn with bright, thick thread, and there are metal rivets at the corners of the pockets and elsewhere. "Where did you get those? What are they called?"

"I don't know what they are called. Levi Strauss makes them and sells them to workingmen from his store. They are supposed to last a long time. That's why I bought them. But I don't think they have a special name."

You go to the Strauss store, a small shop with a bigger workroom behind it. It has actually become something of a little factory. You speak to Mr. Strauss and ask him if he needs another worker. In fact, he does, and you find employment putting the rivets in his pants. During the years, you are given more responsibility, supervising other workers. You spend your entire working life with Levi Strauss, making sturdy pants to outfit America's working people. In a small way, you have been a pioneer, helping to open up this great country, and that makes you very content.

END

119

As your business increases, you and Rosenwald cannot keep up with the demand. Your regional sales representatives send in order after order, and you must hire more people just to fill these requests.

One evening at Rosenwald's dinner table, his son, Julius, tells of an interesting conversation. "Today, a man named Richard Sears came into our clothing store and ordered fifty men's suits. He told me he was going to sell them to customers in Minnesota and Iowa on a mail-order basis. His business sounds a lot like ours, only bigger. He and his partner, Alvah Roebuck, want to expand—they need a bigger warehouse to do more business—but they don't have enough money. I think we could trade *Sears* and *Roebuck* the suits they've ordered for a share of their business. That would free their own funds for expansion. How do you like the idea?"

Rosenwald turns to his son: "Julius, you're absolutely right. We think you are now old enough to run such a business. The two of us are old men. So, you can be a partner in this new enterprise. Go and do it. By the way, what do you propose to call it?"

Julius smiles quietly. "I knew you'd both like the idea. I suppose we shall have to use the names of *Sears* and *Roebuck* for a while, but that's no problem. Someday, I plan to own the business myself, and then we can change the name to Rosenwald and Son!"

END

120

St. Joseph, Missouri, on the western edge of civilization as you know it, is the beginning of the famous Oregon-California Trail. Almost every day, a wagon train leaves for the West. Mules bray; people shout their goodbyes and cry at the thought of never seeing their families again; dust rises; and off they go, headed for dreams and adventure, Indians, mountains, the Pacific Ocean, and always hopes for a better life.

For a while, you resist the temptation to join them. There are great dangers during the trek westward. Reports have come back of entire wagon trains massacred by Indians, and of disease and death. These reports make the rosy visions for the future a little less encouraging.

Still, you have come this far. Why not finish the journey? Why not take the risks? Slowly, you overcome your hesitations and sign up for a place on the next wagon train. You wanted a new life and excitement. Now, you are about to find it.

Turn to page 32.

121

In Europe, Jews had not been allowed to own large pieces of land. Because the laws of many countries had forced them to live in cities and towns, they had never learned to become farmers.

As years pass, you frequently wonder if Jews, given a fair chance, might become pretty good farmers. After all, you think, there is nothing really different about us, except that we never have had the chance to learn. If I were to invest in a large farm outside Chicago and settle some of the new Eastern European Jewish immigrants on it, perhaps we could succeed. It would be a great experiment.

A number of Jews actually accept your offer and begin to learn the skills of farming. Then, something strange and unexpected happens. The city of Chicago grows rapidly. The farmland that you bought outside the city is now surrounded by houses, streets, shops, schools; you own a valuable piece of real estate inside the city itself.

The Jews who tried to learn farming are actually relieved to be part of familiar city life again. Your experiment may not have turned out the way you expected, but you have a golden opportunity. You build houses on your property and sell them. You remember a phrase from an ancient *midrash,* a pun on part of Isaiah 54:13. *Verav shalom bonaiyich,* "Great shall be the peace of your builders." Your life has turned out well; you are at peace.

E N D

122

"You can't fight city hall," they say. "One person cannot change the system. Just accept reality and go about your own business."

You cannot accept this idea. After all, the Bible tells you: "You may not stand idly by while the blood of your neighbor is spilled." [Leviticus 19:16] You are convinced that you must do something to help. But what?

What you can do is extend credit at your store and keep your prices as low as possible. If you can offer these people an alternative place to shop and a chance to stay out of debt to the greedy mining companies, perhaps a slow change will occur. Maybe some of their children will be able to stay in school, learn, and move on to better jobs. Maybe, over time, the power of the companies will be diminished, and the workers will be able to improve the conditions under which they work. It will take time, lots of time, but maybe something will actually change.

As you sit in the synagogue on the afternoon of *Yom Kippur,* the Torah reader chants your favorite verse. You close your eyes and pray: "God, I have tried to be faithful to what You expect of us. I have not stood idly by. I have tried to help. I hope what I have done is acceptable to You. Amen."

END

123

Aha! you think to yourself. Cigars. If everyone of these working men smokes one or two cigars each day—and there are lots of workers in Cleveland, more every day—somebody must make the cigars and sell them to the workers. What a great idea! You will go to work in a cigar factory.

At first, you are given the job of chopping the tobacco leaves into small shreds; this is the tobacco for the inside of the cigar. Dust from the tobacco fills your nose and lungs, and you need to go outside often to sneeze and cough. It cannot be very healthy working like this, but it's a job. You keep your eyes open and watch how the other workers roll large leaves around the chopped tobacco. When one of these other workers cannot continue her work because her breathing is so difficult from years of inhaling tobacco dust, you take her place. Rolling cigars is a little easier than chopping tobacco, although the dust is still everywhere.

If you decide eventually to buy the cigar factory in order to use your profits to open up another opportunity for yourself, turn to page 68.

If you decide to continue working in the cigar factory, unable to risk losing your wages, turn to page 99.

124

That evening as you have dinner with your family, you think aloud: "For years now, I have been in the cigar business. I guess that people have been coughing and getting sick all along. What shall I do?"

"It's very simple, Father," your teenage daughter responds. "You've got to find a way to take care of these sick people."

With the help of many of your friends, you rent a small building and open a hospital. Mount Sinai is a hospital with *kosher* food, a visiting rabbi, and Jewish doctors and nurses. Jewish patients will feel comfortable and safe in such a hospital. But you insist on one special thing: The money you give will go for a section of the hospital that will treat people with breathing problems. At least you will have done something with your money to make the life of other people easier and healthier than it was in the past.

E N D

125

Y ears pass. You continue your practice of generously helping the working men and women of the town, offering them
credit at your hardware store and making it possible for
them and their families to live good lives. They know that
you are Jewish, but no one has ever said anything negative
about that. They are grateful to have you as a good neighbor.

One day, you see a crowd gathering outside your store.
What do you suppose they want? you ask yourself. Perhaps
someone has convinced them that it is wrong for a Jew to
become wealthy on the hard labor of honest Christian workers. You've heard of other Jewish merchants whose stores
were burned down after mobs attacked them for this reason.

When you look out the front window, however, you are
shocked. One of the leading citizens of the city is carrying
a sign: "We Want You for Mayor." Another sign reads: "An
Honest Person for an Honest Job." You end your life as an
honored and respected leader in Circleville. It's been a long
trip from Neustadt, but a wonderful one.

END

126

You join Caesar Kaskel and some others in a protest delegation. Traveling up the river to Cincinnati, then on the railroad all the way to Washington, D.C., you arrange for a meeting with none other than President Abraham Lincoln. When you are ushered into his presence, Kaskel speaks: "Mr. President, we are grateful for all you have done for us in the past. Now, something terrible has occurred. General Grant has issued this order [he pulls a copy out of his pocket] that is so full of prejudice and hatred that we cannot believe you are aware of it. Mr. President, is this order issued with your consent?"

Lincoln reads the order quickly and then summons his secretary. "I want you to give an order to General Halleck, chief of staff of the army. Tell him that this order violates everything that America stands for. It is immediately annulled; from this moment on, it has no force whatsoever."

Immensely grateful to President Lincoln and to the Jews of Evansville, you return to that Ohio River city. Where else would you want to spend the rest of your life except among such proud and dedicated Jews! So, you become a leader in the Jewish community of Evansville, and you never, ever regret that choice.

END

127

Your worst nightmares are realized. The number of injured and killed at the Battle of Shiloh is appalling. You operate on wounded men, hardly stopping for three days straight. You can barely see, you are so tired, and blood covers your handsome uniform. But their pain forces you to continue. Then, one afternoon, as you step out of the hospital tent, you hear a loud and strange sound. A stray cannonball comes flying toward you. You have only a fraction of a second to duck. . . . Not enough. The cannonball strikes you above your left knee, smashing your leg. You know enough about orthopedic medicine to recognize that your only chance is to have the leg amputated, and that is what happens.

You return to Cincinnati, now a wounded hero, and resume your medical practice. A wooden leg helps you walk around, but you will always be disabled. Something good comes of the injury, however. The medical school asks you to teach there, to share your experiences and skills with younger doctors. Although your leg always hurts, some benefit has come from your pain, and you are satisfied.

END

Glossary

Alechem hashalom · May they rest in peace.

American Israelite · The oldest Jewish weekly in America. Founded in Cincinnati, Ohio, in 1954 by *Isaac Mayer Wise* to spread the principles and teachings of Reform Judaism. An excellent record of American-Jewish history, especially in reference to Jewish immigration from Germany and the development of Reform Judaism.

Anshe Chesed Congregation · Founded in Cleveland in 1842. Name means "people of loving-kindness." Congregation is also known today as Fairmount Temple.

(Kehillat) Anshe Ma'ariv · Founded in Chicago in 1846. Name was intended to be Anshe Ma'arav, "people of the West," but the second word was mistakenly spelled Ma'ariv, meaning "evening prayer." The proper word was soon used. Today, the congregation is known as KAM Isaiah Israel, representing the merger of several synagogues.

Bar Mitzvah · A male Jew who becomes obligated to fulfill the commandments. Also the ceremony for boys at age thirteen, which signifies that they are now considered adults in the Jewish religion.

Baruch Atah Adonai · Hebrew for "Praised are You, O God"; the beginning of many Jewish prayers and blessings.

Bet Din · Rabbinical court that can decide all cases except criminal matters.

Bet Olam · Hebrew for "eternal home"; cemetery.

Bimah · Reading desk on the pulpit of a synagogue.

Bist du a landsman? · Yiddish for "Are you a person from my region?"

B'nai B'rith · Jewish fraternal order founded in 1843. Chapters or lodges were soon established in many cities. Today, it is an international organization.

Board of Delegates of American Israelites · First national organization of Jewish congregations in the United States. Founded in 1859 to defend Jewish rights. Merged with the *Union of American Hebrew Congregations* in 1878.

Chanukah · Eight-day festival celebrating the rededication of the Temple in 165 B.C.E. after the Maccabees defeated its Syrian occupiers; a festival of religious freedom.

Chazan · Cantor who traditionally leads the worship service.

Clemens, Samuel (Mark Twain) (1835–1910) · Journalist, writer, humorist. The quotation cited on page 92 is from "Concerning the Jews," Harper's Magazine, June 1899.

Crown of a good name · "Rabbi Shimon said: 'There are three crowns: the crown of learning, the crown of priesthood, and the crown of royalty. But the *crown of a good name* excels them all.' " (Mishnah, *Pirke Avot* 4:17)

Daven Shacharit · To pray or chant the morning prayer with a swaying motion.

Dayan · Judge of a rabbinical court.

De Leon, David (1816–1872) · Physician, surgeon-general of the Confederacy.

Die Deborah · A German-language newspaper, published by *Isaac Mayer Wise.*

Esprit de corps · A French expression for "spirit" or "enthusiasm."

Fremont, John C. (1813–1890) · Explorer, army officer, politician. Noted for his explorations of the American West.

Gam zu letovah · Hebrew for "This, too, is for good." (Babylonian Talmud, Ta'anit 21a)

Goldwater Brothers · Pioneer Jewish settlers of Arizona. Their descendant, Senator Barry Goldwater, ran for the American presidency in 1964, but lost. He was born a Christian.

Grant, Ulysses S. (1822–1885) · Commanding general of the Grand Army of the Republic (Northern states), especially toward the end of the Civil War; eighteenth president of the United States.

Great shall be the peace of your builders · Isaiah 54:13 reads *verav shalom banyich*, "great shall be the peace of your children." In the Babylonian Talmud, Berachot 64a, the word is deliberately mispronounced as *bonaiyich* [Hebrew was not written with vowels at that time], making the verse read "*great shall be the peace of your builders.*" See *Verav shalom bonaiyich.*

Greeley, Horace (1811–1872) · Journalist. The quotation cited on page 59 is taken from a letter "To Aspiring Young Men," written in 1855.

Gutheim, James K. · Reform rabbi in New Orleans, who sided with the Confederacy and left the United States briefly after 1865 rather than take an oath of loyalty to the Union. Later, he returned to New Orleans.

Havdalah · The Saturday evening service that marks the close of the Sabbath.

High Holy Days · *Rosh Hashanah* and *Yom Kippur.*

Kol Bo · Someone whose job is to do a little bit of everything or one who can do everything.

Kosher · Religiously or ritually proper for use. Usually refers to food that must be prepared in special ways.

Kuhn, Loeb, and Company · A major investment banking company founded in 1867 by Abraham Kuhn and Solomon Loeb, who had begun their careers as clothing merchants in Cincinnati, Ohio.

Landsman · A person from the same region as you are. When someone asks if another is a *landsman,* the idea is to find out if two people or their families come from the same place.

Leeser, Isaac (1806–1868) · Jewish leader, educator, journalist, writer. Though not ordained, functioned as rabbi of Congregation Mikveh Israel in Philadelphia.

Lox · Smoked salmon, a delicacy favored by Jews from *Ashkenazic* background.

Melamed · Teacher in a Jewish school, especially an elementary school.

Menken, Adah Isaacs (1835–1868) · Internationally famous actress and poet, who received an enthusiastic reception when she toured the American West.

Midrash · A vast body of literature, generally nonlegal, dealing with philosophy, theology, ethics, folkways, and anecdotes. Most collections are dated from the third to the tenth centuries C.E.

Minhag · The traditional style in which services are conducted in a particular synagogue or community.

Minyan · The minimum ten men required to conduct a traditional Jewish service.

Mitzvah · Hebrew word meaning "God's commandment." Usually used to mean a "good deed."

Mohel · Ritual circumciser.

Negroes · A term for members of the African branch of the black race. Now replaced by the terms Blacks or African Americans.

New York Times · A struggling newspaper in New York City bought by *Adolph S. Ochs* in 1896. *Ochs* promised to offer "All the

News That's Fit to Print" and soon made the paper into one of America's greatest newspapers.

Noah, Mordecai Manuel (1785–1851) · Editor, politician, playwright, diplomat, early Zionist.

Occident · Newspaper edited and published by *Isaac Leeser.*

Ochs, Julius (1826–1888) and Adolph (1858–1935) · Chattanooga, Tennessee, family prominent in journalism. Adolph became the publisher of the *New York Times,* making it one of the most famous newspapers in the world today.

Ophir · Biblical land, possibly in Africa or Arabia, noted for gold. Many references in the Bible. (See I Chronicles 29:4 or Psalms 45:10.)

Pesach seder · The religious service and meal celebrating Passover. *Pesach* is Hebrew for "Passover," the holiday commemorating the Exodus from Egypt.

Pidyon Shevuyim · Redemption or rescue of captives. In Judaism, to ransom or redeem Jews held captive by non-Jews is a *mitzvah.*

Pirke Avot · The section of the Babylonian Talmud that describes proper conduct and stresses Torah study and the observance of the commandments.

Rosh Hashanah · The Jewish new year; one of the two *High Holy Days.* (See Leviticus 23:24 and Numbers 29:1.)

Rothschilds · Family of Jewish financiers founded by Mayer Amschel Rothschild (1744–1812) in Germany and later extending to Great Britain and France and other countries. An image that refers to people of great wealth.

Ruth · A book of the Bible.

Sears, Roebuck, and Co. · The R.W. Sears Watch Co. was founded in 1886 in North Redwood, MN, to sell inexpensive time pieces. It moved to Chicago the next year and was joined by Roebuck. In 1895, Julius Rosenwald and his brother-in-law, Aaron Nusbaum, acquired half of the company, and, by 1908, Rosenwald was the sole owner of this business that became the world's leader in catalog and mail-order merchandising.

Seder · See *Pesach seder.*

Sephardic/Ashkenazic · *Sephardic* Jews come originally from Mediterranean countries. *Ashkenazic* Jews are generally from northern European areas.

Shabbat · Hebrew for "Sabbath."

Shabbos · Yiddish for "Sabbath."

Shalom · Hebrew for "peace"; also used as a greeting.

Shochet · Ritual slaughterer for *kosher* meat.

Shul · Yiddish for "synagogue."

Simchat Torah · Festival of rejoicing over the Torah, when the reading in the synagogue finishes the Book of Deuteronomy and begins again immediately with the Book of Genesis. It comes a day after the end of the *Sukot* festival.

Straus, Lazarus · Pioneer Jewish businessman whose sons later developed R.H. Macy & Co. as America's leading department store.

Sukah · Hebrew for "booth."

Sukot · The harvest festival described in Leviticus 23:33–36 and often called the Festival of Booths or Tabernacles.

Sutro, Adolph (1830–1898) · Mining engineer and financier, who had a reputation for persistence, inventiveness, and concern for the workers. Served two years as mayor of San Francisco.

Tzedakah · Hebrew for "charity."

Union of American Hebrew Congregations · Founded in 1873 by *Isaac Mayer Wise* in Cincinnati; now the central organization of over 800 Reform Jewish congregations in the United States and Canada.

Verav shalom bonaiyich · See *Great shall be the peace of your builders.*

Vestry · "Board of the synagogue"; the word is no longer used in that way.

We should be kind to strangers · "You shall not oppress a stranger. You know the heart of a stranger [how it feels to be a stranger] for you were strangers in the land of Egypt." (Exodus 23:9)

Wise, Isaac Mayer (1819–1900) · Rabbi, journalist. Founder of all the major institutions of Reform Judaism in the United States: *Union of American Hebrew Congregations,* Hebrew Union College, Central Conference of American Rabbis.

Yiddish · A language consisting of medieval German, Hebrew, and Slavic words, which became the daily language of most European Jews.

Yom Kippur · The Day of Atonement; one of the two *High Holy Days.* The most solemn occasion on the Jewish calendar, a day of fasting and repentance.

Suggestions for Further Reading and Study

Birmingham, Stephen. *Our Crowd: The Great Jewish Families of New York*. New York: Harper & Row, 1967.

Cohen, Naomi. *Encounter with Emancipation: The German Jews in the United States, 1830–1914*. Philadelphia: Jewish Publication Society of America, 1984.

Eisenberg, Azriel, ed. *Eyewitnesses to American Jewish History*. 4 vols. New York: Union of American Hebrew Congregations, 1976–1982.

Evans, Eli N. *The Provincials: A Personal History of the Jews of the South*. New York: Atheneum, 1973.

Feingold, Henry L. *Zion in America: The Jewish Experience from Colonial Times to the Present*. New York: Twayne Publisher Inc., 1974.

Karp, Abraham J., ed. *The Jewish Experience in America*. 5 vols. Waltham, Massachusetts: American Jewish Historical Society and New York: Ktav Publishing House, 1969.

Korn, Bertram W. *American Jewry and the Civil War*. Philadelphia: Jewish Publication Society of America, 1951.

Libo, Kenneth, and Howe, Irving. *We Lived There Too: In Their Own Words and Pictures—Pioneer Jews and the Westward Movement of America, 1630–1930*. New York: St. Martin's/Marek Press, 1984.

Marcus, Jacob Rader. *Memoirs of American Jews, 1775–1865*. 3 vols. Philadelphia: Jewish Publication Society of America, 1956.

———. *United States Jewry, 1776–1865*. 4 vols. anticipated; see especially vol. II, "The Germanic Period." Detroit: Wayne State Press, 1991.

Perlman, Robert. *Bridging Three Worlds: Hungarian-Jewish Americans, 1848–1914.* Amherst: University of Massachusetts Press, 1991.

Rochlin, Harriet and Fred. *Pioneer Jews: A New Life in the Far West.* Boston: Houghton Mifflin Co., 1984.

Roseman, Kenneth. *The Melting Pot: An Adventure in New York.* New York: Union of American Hebrew Congregations, 1985.

Winegarten, Ruthe, and Schechter, Cathy. *Deep in the Heart: The Lives and Legends of Texas Jews, a Photographic History.* Austin, Texas: Eakin Press, 1990.

You may also want to consult books about the history of specific Jewish communities. They will be listed in library catalogs by city, state, or name of synagogue.

Other Resources
Adult education programs are offered by various congregations and communities. Local and state Jewish historical societies and archives also offer courses and collections of interesting books and documents.

American Jewish Archives
3101 Clifton Avenue
Cincinnati, Ohio 45220

American Jewish Historical Society
2 Thornton Road
Waltham, Massachusetts 02154

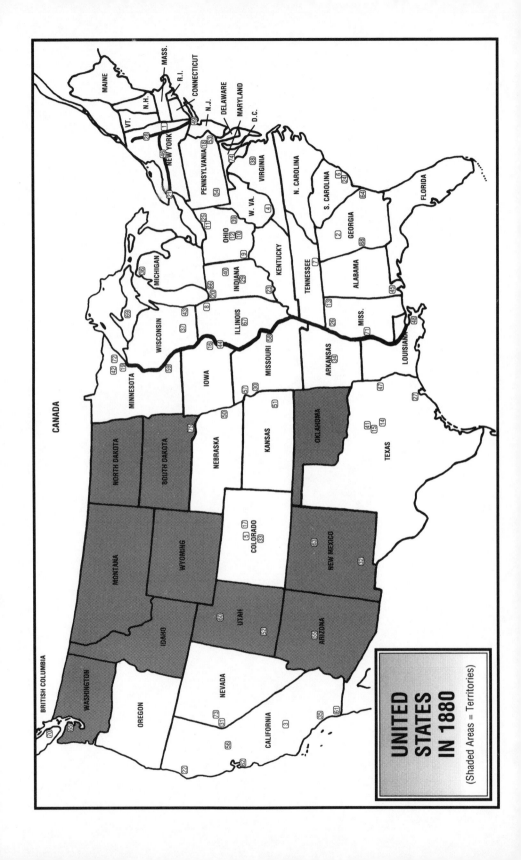

UNITED STATES IN 1880

(Shaded Areas = Territories)

Map Key—United States and Canada

1. Albany, NY
2. Atlanta, GA
3. Bakersfield, CA
4. Bluefield, WV
5. Breckenridge, CO
6. Charleston, SC
7. Chattanooga, TN
8. Chicago, IL
9. Cincinnati, OH
10. Circleville, OH
11. Cleveland, OH
12. Columbus, OH
13. Corinth/Shiloh, MS
14. Corsicana, TX
15. Dallas, TX
16. Davenport, IA
17. Denver, CO
18. Doylestown, PA
19. Duluth, MN
20. East Chicago, IN
21. Erie Canal, NY
22. Eureka, CA
23. Evansville, IN
24. Fort Sumter, SC
25. "The Heights," OH
26. Holly Springs, MS
27. Houston, TX
28. Hudson River, NY
29. Indianapolis, IN
30. Kansas City, MO
31. Lake Tahoe, NV
32. Las Cruces, NM
33. Leadville, CO
34. Little Rock, AR
35. Los Angeles, CA
36. Mackinac, MI
37. Madison, WI
38. Manassas, VA
39. Marietta, OH
40. Marion, IN
41. McKinney, TX
42. Mesabi Range, MN
43. Milwaukee, WI
44. Mississippi River
45. Mobile, AL
46. Mohawk River, NY
47. Nacogdoches, TX
48. New Orleans, LA
49. New York, NY
50. Omaha, NE
51. Osawatomie, KS
52. Parowan, UT
53. Philadelphia, PA
54. Pittsburgh, PA
55. Prescott, AZ
56. Sacramento, CA
57. St. Joseph, MO
58. St. Louis, MO
59. St. Paul, MN
60. Salt Lake City, UT
61. San Diego, CA
62. San Francisco, CA
63. Santa Fe, NM
64. Savannah, GA
65. Seattle, WA
66. South Bend, IN
67. Springfield, IL
68. Talbottom, GA
69. Upper Peninsula, MI
70. Vancouver, BC, Canada
71. Vicksburg, MS
72. Virginia, MN
73. Virginia City, NV
74. Washington, DC
75. Yankton, SD

Important Places Outside North America

1. Bavaria, Germany
2. Berlin, Germany
3. Budapest, Hungary
4. Cape Horn, South America
5. Denmark
6. Finland
7. Floss, Germany
8. Germany
9. Hamburg, Germany
10. Hungary
11. Italy
12. Neustadt, Germany
13. Norway
14. Panama Canal/Isthmus of Panama
15. Poland
16. Posen (Poznam), Poland/Germany
17. Sweden